FATED
TO THE
PHANTOM

INTERNATIONAL BESTSELLING AUTHOR

SARAH SPADE

FOREWORD

Thank you for checking out *Fated to the Phantom*!

This is the fourth book in the **Sombra Demons** series and, like the others, can be read as a standalone. If you have read the other books, though, Sammael has made an appearance in each of the previous ones as the personal mage to Duke Haures, the ruler of Sombra. He was the one who conjured the chains that Nox—the hero of *Stolen by the Shadows*—wears for fourteen years, and he was the mentor to Loki—the hero of *Bonded to the Beast*—before the other demon lost control.

Now, in *Fated to the Phantom*, he finally gets a story! And, of course, you get to meet his librarian heroine, Hope, who has her very own unique reaction to discovering that she's meant for one of these demons. She is a neurodivergent heroine with anxiety and ADHD, but while the mental health rep is there, it's just another part of who she is.

This book also features the fated mates trope, a quick mention of a deceased parent, explicit sex scenes, some profanity, and a ton of instalove. It's specifically written for adult readers who like a little fluff and some spice with their monster romance.

Enjoy :)

xoxo,

Sarah

SAMMAEL

As I watch Loki's mate pass the *Grimoire du Sombra* off to the two-horn, I already can tell there isn't a single thing I won't do to get my claws on that book.

It's the only of its kind in existence, and not just because of how it was kept. In the archives of the School of Mages, very few scrolls are bound in creature skin like the spellbook. And those that are? They are powerful grimoires that only the most elite of mages are allowed to read.

As Duke Haures's personal mage these last few centuries, I have had the opportunity to flip through many of them. As much as I hungered for knowledge, thirsted for power, the only thing I craved more than all is my one true mate.

My female.

My *forever*.

For nine centuries now, I've waited. I've searched. I've *hoped*... and when the sole scroll featuring the ancient matefinder spell was stolen by my prized student only for Loki to fail in the cast and turn fully demonic, I resigned myself to continuing to do the same.

As powerful a mage as I am, I was always taught that magic wouldn't bring me my mate. The only spell that *might*... a manifestation that could possibly search the other realms and planes and even the scattered clans of Sombra for my female... was a myth spoken of in hushed whispers at the School of Mages.

And then, mere decades ago, a portal into Sombra from the human realm of legend opened, summoning Duke Haures before he brought his mortal mate back to our world of shadows. Her name was Susanna, and she was the first to confirm that there was a matefinder spell—the *verus amor* incantation—in the grimoire she left behind.

Duke Haures's first law as the ruler of Sombra is that the human world is off-limits to all demonkind. Since he bonded with his formerly mortal mate, I've been to the human realm on the duke's orders multiple times. Of course. My mage specialty revolves around portal travel and the ability to weave enchanted chains for his enemies and his punishments so it was always my duty, as both his mage and one of his soldiers.

I did what was commanded of me, but I never forgot the promise of Susanna's grimoire. When Nox —a hunter from a poorer clan on the edge of Sombra's shadows—found he was fated to belong to a human spawn who was also Susanna's kin, I was there to put him in his chains. Then, many cycles later, when Malphas—a clan artist from Nuit—was claimed by a pale-haired human. I, along with Glaine, traveled to the human world again and again... but though I hoped to find the book, I never did.

And then Loki—no longer demonic, his empty white gaze blazing its usual purple once more— brought his human female to meet with Duke Haures in Mavro this day.

His mate carried the *Grimoire du Sombra* in her small, pale hands. She first offered it to Duke Haures, who haughtily refused it. He has a mate of his own— though he's still careful to keep Susanna hidden from any and all threats—and no need for the grimoire any longer.

Now that the book is responsible for at least four demon-human pairings, the duke decided that it was firmly human magic. Loki agreed. It needed to return to the human realm so that the charms would lead another mortal to summon their demon or demoness to them.

Loki's mate is already with spawn. He has every intention of keeping her in Sombra, safe and protected in his village. Returning to the human world to bring the book back isn't an option for the two-horn.

Suddenly, from my post standing at the duke's back, I understand why he insisted on Nox and his human mate, Amelia, joining in on this conversation. Having taken the portal from the human realm to Mavro so that Susanna could meet with her kin, Nox and Amelia were meant to return early this morning. Instead, Duke Haures sent his favored soldier to retrieve Loki and his Kennedy from Nuit, then told the other bonded pair to stay.

I was also commanded to visit the palace.

Glaine, on the other claw, faded to shadow once he'd accomplished his task. As much as he prizes being the lead guard for the duke, I know what it costs him to visit Nuit and see Lilith. He'll be stalking around the gardens of Mavro, regretting the choices he made, while I stand here, watching my hopes of my own future slip away as Kennedy gives the book over to Loki.

Protective and possessive, Loki can't allow his expecting mate to approach another male. It matters not that Nox wears Amelia's name branded on his chest the same way Loki bears that of his tiny human female on his. His eyes might be purple now, but there's a touch of darkness that clings to his pair of double horns. If he feels like his claim to his mate is at all threatened, he won't hesitate to ram that threat with those horns.

That's what he did in Nuit, attacking the former clan artist. From Apollyon's reports, Loki has calmed since then, but the way he watches the three males in this room closely, I know that he wouldn't hesitate to act to shield his mate and their future spawn.

I don't want his mate. I want that book because, more than anything in this plane or any other, I simply want *mine*.

It's not even about having a family, either. I'm a selfish enough male that—like Nox and his mate who, after countless gold moons passing, still are without any offspring—I'd be content to solely have my female for my own.

And that book will make sure I find her at last.

From the moment I stumbled upon Duke Haures's dark-haired, white-skinned female in the dungeons—where the duke stored her during the tumultuous early days of their mating—something about her soft features, ridge-free brow, and head absent of any horns... I knew. I simply *knew*. Susanna Benoit was meant for my master, but there would be no Soleil demoness for me.

My mate will be one of the legendary humans.

Forbidden fruit and nearly impossible to find with the duke's first law in effect, if my mate really *is* a human female, not even being his personal mage would save me from his wrath if I break the law that he issued more than two millennia ago.

Humans aren't allowed to know that Sombra exists. That *we* exist. I cannot take a portal and hope that I stumble upon my one true mate because that world is banned for all of my kind, save for when Duke Haures sends us on a mission—or our mates summon us to their realm.

But what if I use the *Grimoire du Sombra* to summon her to *me*?

I have the magic to do so. After centuries of training and experience, there is no one more qualified to read the ancient spells and wield them than I. The matefinder scroll from the archives went missing with Loki over a century ago, long before I chanced on Susanna Benoit and my instincts roared that I, too, would have a human mate. Perhaps I could have wielded that one, but knowing that the book Loki's holding now is responsible for leading *four* of my fellow Sombra demons to find their human mates has me desperate to try the fabled *verus amor* spell.

I need it. I need it more than anything else I've ever needed before, and while I try to keep my features schooled so that none can tell how much I long to snatch the book right from his grip, I understand that

Duke Haures plans on having Nox and his female return the book to the human realm.

Not if I offer first.

Moving out from behind Duke Haures's throne, I turn to Loki. Holding out my hand, I tell him, "I shall take the book."

Everyone in the throne room looks at me.

I straighten my back. "I can travel to the human realm and leave the book behind without being seen. And if I am? I can use magic to make the mortals forget."

Nox rumbles deep in his chest.

His reaction is no surprise. Though we act cordial these days, the hunter has never forgiven the duke for ordering him to spend fourteen human years in the dungeons, Glaine for dragging him beneath the elaborate castle, or me for being the one to clasp him in the enchanted golden chains—or for how I was tasked with taking his human mate's memories of him.

I had to. She was still a human spawn when Nox first found her, and while Duke Haures's first law allows for mates to learn the truth of Sombra, Nox couldn't bond his Amelia to him until she was a mature female. He had to take the chains just like I needed to remove any trace of Sombra from the child.

But the book worked the way it is charmed to, keeping the bond open between them so that Nox could return to her side when she needed him the most. Fully grown and prepared to bond with the hunter, Nox claimed his human—but not without complications.

The way he no longer has control over his dual forms being the most noticeable.

I'm responsible for that, too. Or, rather, the chains I conjured are. Still wearing them when Nox ripped open a hole between realms, he fed nearly all of his essence into the chains to break free of their bonds. Now, instead of choosing whether he's red-skinned and solid or transparent as his shadows, Nox flips between the two. He's allowed to stay in the human world so long as no one sees him, and I'm not wrong when I say that it would be less risky for me to go with the book even without my mage abilities.

Duke Haures leans back on his throne, pale hands laid casually on the arms of his crystalline chair. The blue tint from Mavro's oasis matches his glowing gaze, coloring his white skin, his long white hair, and his bottom tusks.

I'm a mage. Not a two-horn, like Loki, but born with the gift of magic, made obvious by my purple eyes. Duke Haures? He's... he's something else, and not only because he is the only pale-skinned demon in Sombra. He exhales magic with every breath, barely contained violence in each inch of his huge body.

As my gaze slides over to the duke, I know instantly that he suspects that my motives aren't pure at all.

I nod at him anyway. "It was once the property of the School of Mages," I remind him. "This might be human magic now, but I should still be the one to handle it."

Duke Haures steeples his claws. "I trust you, Sammael," is all he says before he nods regally toward Loki. "Give the book to my mage."

Loki only hesitates long enough to trail one of his shadowy hands down his mate's arm before he stalks toward me, thrusting the book out.

I take it, but Loki doesn't let go straight away.

"Be careful," he murmurs under his breath instead. "We both know better than to play with old magic."

He isn't wrong. An entire century in the shadows, existing as a full demon because he casted a spell he wasn't ready for... my former student learned more with one failed spell than all of his lessons.

So did I. Because I?

I will *not* fail.

CHAPTER 1
PHANTOM

SAMMAEL

Nodding at Loki, I tug on the book. He releases it, then returns to stand at his mate's side.

Perhaps I am too eager. With the tips of my claws digging into the edge of the binding, the book in my possession at last, I gesture with my left hand. The moment the portal to the human realm appears in front of me, I walk right into it.

I trust you…

Duke Haures's words are echoing through my head as I touch down among the shadows of a dingy corner of the human realm. The scents—more earthy and oily and bitter than the waters of Mavro or the fiery ash of the rest of Sombra—make it clear to me that I've crossed planes.

I'm sure the duke expects me to set the book down, relying on the magic inside of it to find the next human it's destined for, then return to Sombra.

I don't. I *can't*. I'm willing to sacrifice his trust in me for the chance of summoning my mate.

And that's what I am going to do.

I have the book. I'm in the human realm so the veil between worlds won't keep me from her. All I have to do is manifest her, then give her the mate's promise to mark her as mine. Once she does the same, I have until the first gold moon to convince her to accept me as her forever mate, and then it won't matter that I betrayed Duke Haures.

For a chance at my forever, I'd do that and more.

As a shadow, I can control how much of my body appears before I melt into the darkness surrounding me. Right now, I'm so faded that no one peering down the alley would see me at all. With the book nestled on top of my bent knees, crouching down to the strange packed dirt of this world, it disappears with the rest of me.

I can still see it. Waving my hand over the front cover, the pages flip until they stop on the only spell I need.

Verus amor.

The true love incantation.

With the exception of two words scrawled in ink in the strange human lettering, the rest is printed in Sombran. The second part of the spell is the mate's promise that every mature Sombra demon knows instinctively, but the first part...

My eyes gleam in excitement, lighting up the yellowed page as I begin to read the manifestation spell out loud.

The wind picks up halfway through the cast, sending my long hair whipping around my face. Usually, the elements don't affect me when I'm in my shadow form, but this isn't a normal wind. This is magic, and I have to brace my claws in the earth to keep from being knocked over as I finish the spell.

I immediately launch into the mate's promise, the vows—"My soul will be yours... my heart is in your hands..."—getting lost in the wind as I finish offering everything I am, everything I will be to the single female meant for me.

Now, I went into this cast understanding that there was a chance it would fail if only because my mate does not exist just yet. Another reason why human mates are as revered as they are considered forbidden fruit is how they are not immortal like my kind. At nine centuries old myself, she could have been born and lost long before I even knew to be searching for her. Perhaps she isn't even born yet. My wait might have to continue—

—and then something happens and, one way or another, I know that the spell at least *took*.

Instead of whipping around me, the unnatural wind cuts right through me. It slices through my innards, it stabs at my heart, it seizes all of the breath from my lungs before it bursts free from my eyes, momentarily blinding me.

The dark consumes me. I lose all direction, only knowing that I'm falling for a split second before the wind lifts me up, grabbing me, pulling me away from the alleyway and into a portal that is not mine.

The last thing I hear is the thud of the now solid book hitting the ground before I'm swallowed up by the wind.

***

TIME LOSES ALL MEANING AS I WHIRL BEFORE, SUDDENLY, I'm being flung forward and, the wind finally dying down, I'm standing on my feet.

The first thing I notice once I am is that I have not left the human realm. More than that, wherever I am, I'm indoors now.

The space has a bed, furniture made from wood, and a large oval piece of reflective glass that shows the room in reverse. Not a scrying mirror like we keep in the School of Mages, but something similar.

And there, in the center of the bedding, is a slumbering human female.

Her hair is as dark as her skin is fair. Her features are elfin rather than the strong nose and jaw belonging to a demoness. She smells of something slightly sweet and faintly milky, and from my first inhale, everything in me stills.

"Oh." I shudder out a breath at the sight of the beauty lying on her back. "Was ever a male as lucky as I?"

She doesn't react, and I raise my voice a little more so as to wake her gently.

I'm in my shadow form in case I frighten her with my much larger, different appearance. Though I don't worry that I will. All of the human females who were fated for a Sombran demon seem quite pleased with their males.

So shall my mate.

I already find her *exquisite.*

"For nine centuries, I dreamed of this moment," I breathe out. "Won't you wake, my mate, so I can see the color of your eyes?"

In Sombra, we all have bright, shining eyes, but the color gives us an insight into what a demon or demoness will grow to be. Those with purple are destined to be mages, while green belongs to the soldiers and the guards. Gold is usual for the craftsmen, while red is meant for those who hunt and kill, such as Nox.

I've met enough humans to know that their eyes don't glimmer like ours, and that the color is just a color. But my female... I want to know everything about her—and that begins with seeing what color her eyes are.

She doesn't stir for a few moments, but when she makes the most adorable snuffling sound as she does, similar to one I've heard from the ungez, I hold my breath in anticipation and wait.

Taking mercy on her male, she comes to quickly, rising up enough that she can glance around the dim shadows that fill her space.

Her eyes land on me.

My heart leaps to see that they're the same shade as Duke Haures.

"Beautiful and powerful," I whisper reverentially. "As if I had any doubts that you were born to be mine."

She frowns, her smooth forehead furrowing. Then, in the human language I don't yet understand, she says, "Isomm wondere?"

Her gaze slides away from me.

Hm. Am I too hidden in the lingering shadows for her to locate me?

I try to shift to my solid form so that she can't miss me—and that doesn't seem to work, either.

How odd.

"It is I," I tell her in Sombran, raising my voice more as I drift toward the side of her bedding. "Sammael. Your one true mate."

Leaning up on her elbow, she runs her fingers through her soot-colored hair. She's squinting into the shadows, and for a moment I have hope that she sees me until she yawns and shifts against her bedding before lying on her back.

"Ograte. Mseein tings'gain," she mumbles, more to herself than to me.

Because she... she's not talking to me. For some terrible reason, she has no idea that I've joined her in her quarters.

Then, turning on her side and suddenly reaching out, she shoves her hand right through me as though I am not here and I have to admit that my suspicions are right.

Gasping at the intrusion, I'm too stunned to react. This... this isn't common. As a shadow, the edges of my form aren't solid at all, but no matter how I appear, no one should be able to move through me like she just did.

And then she does it again.

She's holding a glass-covered rectangle in her hand now. She must have reached through me to grab it from the wooden stand at my back. Tapping it with her dull fingertip, she squints at the rectangle.

"Stillave anower toosleep," she murmurs before

tossing the rectangle down on her bedding, closing her eyes before it even falls.

"My mate," I call, desperation having my rumble come out as a pained cry.

There's no reaction from her, though a shout like that should have been enough for anyone in the room to hear.

Not my female.

She cozies up with her covering, sighing peacefully as she returns to her slumber.

Because... because she can't see me. She can't hear me.

And I? I cannot touch her.

No matter how I try, I stay transparent. My solid form is still gone and so, it seems, is my magic. I wave my see-through hands, gesturing with my claws, pleading with as much essence as I can spare to open a portal to bring me back to Sombra... and nothing happens.

I don't want to leave my female. But I need to return to Sombra to figure out how to reverse what the spell has done to me because, otherwise, she will never *be* my female—and, yet, I cannot.

It's as though I'm closed off from my home world, a mournful demon who found his true love only to have the promise of his mate thrust in front of him, then taken away just as quickly.

I found her, but she does not know. In this form, as

she proved as she passed right through me, I cannot touch her the way a Sombran must to trigger our bond or begin an essence exchange... and all that means one thing.

I'm not fully demonic, not like Loki, but the old magic made me pay for my hubris in a different way.

I am a *phantom*.

Worse, I'm a phantom trapped in the human realm with an unaware female—and because I left it behind and can no longer open a portal like I always have, the *Grimoire du Sombra* is once again out of my reach.

CHAPTER 2
DEPOSITORY

HOPE

FOUR MONTHS LATER

How do you know if you're going crazy?

That's what I'm wondering today as I shelve books at work. Because, when I turn down one of the furthest stacks of the library and something about the shape of the shadows welling in the corner has me swallowing an *eep* before jamming the book on its shelf and scurrying away, I can't deny it any longer.

I honestly think something is wrong with me—and more than the usual anxiety and tendency to overthink that I've struggled with my entire life.

If it was just the shadows that spooked me, I could blame it on my watching horror movies at a young age with Johanna and inevitably screwing up my psyche. Can't deny that I have. I might be twenty-eight, but I purposely chose to rent a home that didn't have a basement or an attic because they've made me nervous for as long as I can remember.

I'm a bit of a scaredy-cat, too, I admit it, and it's only gotten worse since this strange feeling that I'm being... I don't know... like, *followed,* kind of, has settled over me like a shadow of doom or something.

I can't explain it. For the last few months—maybe since early summer—I can't shake the sensation that someone's watching me. Out of the corner of my eye, I swear I see someone melting into the shadows, but there's never anyone there when I turn to get a better look.

My name is a whisper on a breeze that I try to convince myself I don't hear.

And then there's the way that, despite living alone, my house doesn't feel as... as *empty* as it used to.

This is where the crazy comes into play. Because, logically, I know that no one is out there stalking me. Why would they? I have a good relationship with nearly all of my exes, and considering I've been single since me and Corey decided on an amicable split two years ago, I don't think it's any of them.

Besides, lately I don't really go anywhere except

home, work, and for the occasional meal out with Johanna and her husband so it's not like I managed to pick up a stalker or something like that.

And yet... I just don't know. The feeling hasn't gone away, and I have to work to shake off my recent scare as I head back to the counter to check the depository for returned library books.

Today, I'm working alongside two other librarians: Jake Reynolds, who is a library clerk like me, and Moira Cooke, our library technician and the head of the Westfield Library.

Our library is made up of a staff of seven full-time employees, including our janitor, with about as many part-time workers and volunteers. As a clerk, it's my job to shelve, process, and check out library materials, though I'm in the running for taking over as a library assistant when Victoria retires at the end of the year.

Without a diploma or any certification, it's the most I can hope for right now. One day, when I can afford it, I'd like to go back to school and get my degree in library sciences, but when the choice came down to getting loans or jumping in with two feet into the workforce, I didn't really have a choice. As it is, I barely scrape by with enough to pay my rent and come out with a couple dollars extra at the end of the month.

It's worth it, though. I've always loved books and knew I wanted to spend my life surrounded by them. I'm firmly child-free—though I love my sister's kids like they're my own—and while I'm still searching for the perfect partner for me, my first love is books. Whether those in the library or my own never-ending TBR, my life revolves around books, and any guy who wants to settle down with me has to understand that.

Speaking of...

"Hey, Hope! I didn't know you were working today."

Funny that I knew that *he* was on shift. Probably because I got the same schedule e-mailed to me that he did so I know who I'll see on any given shift at the library.

Jake Reynolds is one of the only two men who work at the library; the other is Paulie, our janitor. He's a cute guy a couple of years younger than me, with a dimple in his chin, messy dark curls, and pretty brown eyes hidden behind a pair of wire-rimmed frames. He has a tan even now in October, and a tendency to wear tight henley shirts every shift to show off his lanky yet undeniably muscular build.

I blame myself for that. Not really thinking about it, I innocently complimented his shirt shortly after he started working with us last spring. Now, I've always been a bit oblivious. It takes a lot before I realize that someone is flirting with me instead of just being friendly, and I would've thought that Jake would be more into the younger co-eds who work part-time at the library. There's Liza and Jennifer, both leggy and gorgeous, and even sweet Samantha who turns beet-red whenever Jake grins.

We don't have any kind of policy when it comes to dating co-workers, probably because our profession skews heavily toward women, and the men who craft the policies seem to forget that lesbians and other sexualities apart from hetero exist. But despite the other girls all trying to catch Jake's attention, he seems to be stuck on me.

Having him ask me out for dinner and drinks kind of made it obvious, especially when he clarified that he was hoping it would be a date. A way for the two of us to get to know each other outside of the library.

I turned him down gently, mainly because—to put it bluntly—I don't shit where I eat. If I hooked up with Jake and it all went wrong, things would be awkward at work. I like my job. I don't want to start over at another branch because I couldn't keep my panties on. He's cute, and I'd be lying if I said I wasn't attracted to him, but I have my job and my bills to consider.

He took it well, and we both came to a silent understanding not to bring it up again... but then I think about the henleys and the way he deliberately brushes against me behind the counter and how excited he is to be on a shift with me and... yeah. We're friends for now, but the moment I give him any sign that I'd like to become *more* than friends, I'm pretty sure he'll jump at the chance.

I almost want to try Jake on for size. I think we'd be a good match, and Lord knows I've been giving my battery-operated boyfriend a workout since ending things with Corey, but... I don't know. Any time I almost give in, I second-guess myself.

Not like I don't do that always anyway, huh?

Welcome to being Hope McReary, I guess.

As I move behind the counter, he sets down his phone. I pretend not to notice. I'm not in charge, and if he wants to risk Moira snapping at him to stay off his phone while he's working the counter, that's his problem.

Until he says, "Did you hear about what happened to Whiskey Rose? I know you're a fan."

Now that? *That* catches my attention.

I thought he would bring up the recent rush of break-ins that Westfield has been dealing with lately. Six in the last three weeks that I know of, and as a community staple, nearly all of our patrons—and most of the staff—have been talking about it since the third one.

Instead, he mentioned Whiskey Rose.

Am I a fan? Yeah. That's putting it mildly.

Whiskey Rose is one of my favorite singers, something that anyone who spends any time around me at all knows almost instantly. A bonafide pop star who emerged on the scene when I was in my early teens, she constantly tops the streaming sites, starred in a big blockbuster film last summer and another come next year, and recently launched the American leg of her world tour... and I can sing any song from her four albums with barely any prompting.

I even have one of the lyrics from her breakout hit tattooed around my ankle: *in this world of stardust*, from "Heart Barely Used". Little twinkling stars are inked in a pale purple around the black script, a reminder for me that, no matter how hard life gets and how often my heart feels bruised, there's still magic in this world.

I have tickets to see her at Metlife Stadium in three months. It'll be my first time seeing her live and I probably spent more than I should've on my nosebleed seats.

If my status as superfan is up-to-date, she's currently on the West Coast, touring California after *Jessica's Journey* came out in June. But unless something happened since I've been at work, I have no idea what he's talking about.

Whiskey Rose is in the news a lot, and I pay attention; you could say she's one of my hyperfixations. I know everything about Whiskey. The biggest pop star of my generation, I even loved her when she was part of Thr33peat, and when she left the group and started releasing solo albums. She's what you would call 'America's sweetheart', and there was a time when she was part of the biggest power couple in pop music.

Whiskey and Jared Turner broke up when I was in

high school. She's been cruising on her own ever since, and considering a crazed fan confronted her last summer, pulling a gun on her when she was out promoting her first movie role, I don't blame her for keeping her private life private.

So, yeah. I'm a superfan, but I'm nowhere near as obsessed as that weirdo. Still, Jake's got my attention, and I have to know.

So I ask.

"What? What happened to her?"

"Her voice broke."

I blink. "What? Are you kidding? Is that even possible?"

"I guess so. They're already talking about her having to cancel part of her tour. Seems her voice cracked or something, then she started freaking out on stage. They're calling it nodules, saying she needs vocal rest, but that doesn't explain the freak-out, if you ask me."

I still don't get it.

"What do you mean, 'freak-out'?"

"It's all over the internet. Here. I'll show you." Jake grabs his phone, entering his passcode. "There were so many cameras at the show they couldn't keep it quiet. It went viral."

Now, I know better than to get caught up in looking at Jake's phone. Moira has a sixth sense when it comes to her staff messing around on their devices when we have patrons in the library, and she proves it by walking out of the children's library section a moment later, marching right over to the counter where Jake and I have our heads bowed over his phone.

"*Ahem.*"

Shit!

Jake jabs the pause button almost immediately after the roar of the crowd and Whiskey Rose's signature rasp turns into a high-pitch scream before cracking, then dying. I scoot away from him, as though putting a couple of feet between us will convince Moira that I wasn't watching his phone, too.

Moira is usually a sweet woman in her mid-fifties —until she catches her librarians on their phones. When she does, her face gets this pinched look that I remember vividly from my second-grade teacher. Mrs. Haley *hated* eight-year-old Hope for no good reason that I can think of except for maybe my tendency to throw up whenever it was time to take our spelling test, but still. I hated getting in trouble then as much as I do now as an adult.

"Sorry, Moira," I say sheepishly as Jake's phone disappears as if by magic. "I was just going to check the depository."

She sniffs, slightly mollified. "I thought I heard a book being returned before. Be a dear, Hope, and check it in if it has."

"On it."

"And you, Jake? Isn't this the second time I've had to talk to you about your phone this week? Tell me... what's so important that you had to distract Hope with it?"

"Oh, um... you see—"

Whoops. I leave Jake to figure out how to explain about Whiskey Rose while I quickly cross over to the other side of the library, aiming for the depository.

Our depository is basically a chute that leads to the outside of the library. For patrons who find it more convenient to return their books either after hours or without having to come all the way inside, they can drop their library book in the chute and it lands in a padded box on the inside.

It's my job to empty the depository box whenever I'm on an opening shift. There are usually a couple waiting for us in the morning, with plenty coming through as the day goes on.

I already cleaned it out twice today. Crouching down, reaching into the box, I see that there's another entry.

My fingers twitch as they touch the leather of the cover, a jolt of electricity running from the tips down until my whole wrist seems to tingle.

Okay. That was odd.

Shaking out my hand, I grab the book again. It's heavier than I thought it would be. Tightening my grip on it, I lift it up and turn it over so that I can get a good look at the book.

There's a barcode sticker on the back, but it's not one that belongs to Westfield Library. Just like I expected.

Flipping over the book, I see that it has a star embossed in gold on the leather with a circle hitting each point of the star. The leather is pitting, obviously very old, and the book as a whole has a musty scent to it that's like *old book* times a hundred.

I actually kind of like it.

There's no title, though. No author. I open the book, careful not to crack the spine, searching for the title page—and frowning when I see that there is a list of four names written on the inside cover.

Susanna Benoit is scrawled in cursive. The name AMY is a blocky print right under Susanna's; it looks like a child did it in crayon. Beneath that, in a thick pencil, is *Shannon Crewes*, followed by *Kennedy Barnes*.

Weird.

The title page is even weirder. It's done in a thick type-set font, printed deep in the page, and it says the book is called: *Grimoire du Sombra*.

And that's about all it says.

I still don't have an author name. There's no copyright date, no information about who printed it, or anything other than those three words. Flipping through the yellowed pages, going slowly so that I don't tear them, I notice that none of it is in English.

I... I have no idea what language it *is* in, either.

Okay. I need some help.

Walking back to the counter, I see that Jake is missing. My boss probably sent the charming library clerk on break to give herself a few minutes without him being in her face because it's not like anyone ever gets fired here. Not that that stops me from fearing it every other shift, but that's life as Hope for you. I take the worst-case scenario and convince myself that it'll happen every freaking time.

Hopefully this isn't one of them.

"Hey, Moira?"

"Yes?"

Oof. She's still a little short with me. Jake's attempt at an explanation must have ticked her off even more.

Yup. Definitely sent him away for now...which means that I can't even tell her to forget about it and see if he can help me figure this out.

I lift up the book, showing her the cover. "Sorry, but I think we got another freebie."

It's pretty common. People think that, just because we're a library, they can drop off any book and we'll be tickled pink to accept them. They don't understand how often we have to cull shelves just to make room for the books we already have, or that we have strict standards for our material.

Moira holds out her hand. "Let me see."

I give it to her, waiting as she does exactly what I did. She *tuts* when she sees the retail sticker on the back, frowning when she notices that four different people scrawled their names on the inside cover, then closes it, running her finger over the strange design on the front one.

"It's unique," she says at last, "but you're right. It's not one of ours. Still... I think our patrons might find it interesting. Why don't you go ahead and enter it into the system and print a tag for it."

She extends the book back to me.

"Um, sure," I say, accepting it. Only... "Where do you think I should shelve it?"

Moira raises her eyebrows at me. "Where do *you* think it should go, Hope?"

Oh, great. It's a test.

I bite down on my bottom lip, thinking it over. "It says it's a 'grimoire' so that makes me think it belongs with our books on the occult. It's definitely foreign, and since I can't translate it, I'm not sure if it really belongs in the fiction section. Then again, it's really old, obviously, so maybe out of print?"

My boss nods in approval. *Phew.* "Good choices, all of them. But let's go with that first one, shall we?"

The occult. That's what I figured. "Sure thing, Moira. I'll do it right away."

And if I can sneak my phone out of the drawers

where the staff are supposed to keep them while on duty so I can check up on what's going on with Whiskey Rose... well, the occult section is in the back of the library where few patrons rarely go, isn't it?

I just hope the shadows don't startle me again.

CHAPTER 3
GRIMOIRE DU SOMBRA

HOPE

S o, good news first.

After sneakily reading a few articles between the stacks, I'm pretty sure there's a good chance that my concert won't be canceled. Whiskey Rose's reps put out a statement that she's resting privately, will be reevaluated constantly, and is eager to rejoin her tour in the new year.

Even better news: it doesn't look like there was another break-in last night, either.

For some strange reason, Westfield and the neighboring towns of Clark, Edison, and Iselin have all been plagued by home invasions and burglaries since the end of summer. It's mid-October now, and there have even been a few in my part of town, including one in the cul de sac at the end of my street.

I live alone. I don't have the extra cash for an alarm system or even a doorbell camera, though I try to be careful to lock my door behind me whenever I remember to. It doesn't matter. I've been stalking the local news for weeks now, waiting for the cops to announce that they caught the guy or gal responsible so that I don't have to keep fixating on it.

Unfortunately, there's nothing yet, but at least the media coverage might be putting a little pressure on the culprit. It's good to see that no one was burgled last night, and while I know I don't really have anything that a thief would want, that doesn't stop my brain from insisting that I'll eventually be a target.

It's just how I'm wired, I guess. Anxiety is a bitch, and when you add that to my other neurodivergent tendencies, it's a miracle I can make it on my own as it is. Considering I almost burned my house down last winter because I left the gas burner on overnight, even I question myself.

I'm stubborn enough to keep at it, though.

My dad always tells me that I can move back in with him and my stepmom if I want to, and Johanna would turn her husband's office into a guest room for me if I decided to stay with her family, but I like my house. It's something that's *mine* which is probably why I'm so worried about someone breaking into it.

And, of course, there's that strange suspicion I can't shake that it's suddenly *haunted* or something...

My home isn't very big. A narrow two-story house nestled between a row of similar structures, I have a small backyard, a tiny porch, and pale pink shutters on the front that I painted myself so that it stands out from the more natural colors that my neighbors have. There's an oak tree standing proudly between my land and the Wilkins next door, with a mess of orange leaves and scattered acorns everywhere now that it's fall.

I have a whole pumpkin sitting on the far end of my porch, using my summer chair as a perch. If it's still firm by Halloween, I'll carve it; if the unseasonable warmth followed by the rain we just can't seem to shake makes it mushy, I'll chuck it and get another one from the nearby Stop and Shop. We have countless squirrels in our neighborhood, and I've caught one or two eyeing my pumpkin, but it's still untouched, the only decoration I've gotten around to setting out for the impending season.

Speaking of squirrels...

Because my house is within walking distance of the library, I get my steps in when the weather's nice; it saves me gas money, too, leaving my car parked along the street while I stroll to and from the library. It's brisk out today, cooler than it has been, and I'm eager to get back inside where I can warm up since I totally blanked on grabbing a jacket this morning.

Pulling my house keys out of my purse, I'm jogging up the three stairs that lead to my porch when my sneaker falls on a pile of acorns gathered in front of my door. I didn't see them there, and I'm freaking lucky I don't slip and fall backward down the steps, but—*youch*—does that hurt when my instep gets pummeled by the rock-like nuts.

The Westfield squirrels have been working overtime. This isn't the first time I've found acorns strewn across my porch. At first, I wondered if the wind had a way of knocking the acorns loose before they landed on my property, but I've given up trying to figure it out. Squirrels gathering the acorns and abandoning them in front of my door is as good an explanation as any, especially since—no matter how often I get rid of them —there's always more.

Today, I'm not pressed to go inside, grab my broom from my coat closet, and come back to sweep the acorns onto the leaves I keep meaning to rake. And maybe I'm still peeved at the bruise I'm probably going to get along my instep, but I take my annoyance out on the nuts by toeing them off the porch with the tip of my shoe.

There. At least, later, when I leave my house again, I won't have to worry about tripping over these acorns.

Once inside my home, I have to purposely remind

myself to hang my keys on the key hook I installed by my door. If I don't, there's a good chance I'll leave without them, and that's if I don't lose them first. No keys means I won't be able to lock my house. Not a good idea with some unknown burglar creeping around and—with that thought—I purposely lock my front door behind me before kicking off my shoes.

My foot's okay. I detour to my downstairs bathroom to check it out, then do my business since I prefer not to use the library's toilet if I don't have to. After changing from my work clothes to a comfy set of sweats, I put on my favorite pair of memory foam slippers before going to the kitchen to figure out what the hell I'm going to eat for dinner today.

That's the one downside to living on my own. As the only grown-up here, I'm responsible for all of my meals. It's easier when I have a partner—since I usually ask them to take on the mental load of dinner —but when I'm single? That's on me.

And I can only have so much take-out before my local delivery people know me by name and my repeated order du jour...

I'm not in the mood to cook today so I rely on one of my safe foods I keep around for nights like these. When I'm not hyperfixating on one particular meal— like how, last week, I ate barbecue chicken pizza four nights in a row—I fall back on the comfort foods that are quick, easy, and always taste good.

Tonight it's grilled cheese sandwiches and canned soup, and I'm ready to go in less than ten.

Rather than sit at my small, circular kitchen table by myself, I set up a tray table in the living room and eat my dinner in front of the TV.

I've recently splurged for a new streaming service. They're too pricy to have more than one at a time, and after I canceled my Netflix at the beginning of the summer, I decided to try out the Disney one until I got bored with it. I still haven't, and with Halloween coming up, I figure I'll watch all of the specials it has, plus I've always been a sucker for the old Disney classics.

I've been working my way through their repertoire of animated movies. For a few weeks in August, I repeatedly watched the 1953 version of *Peter Pan* before trading it off for my old DVD of the 2003 film with the same name; that one became my sleepy-time show, the same movie I put on before bed so that I can listen to something as I doze off. When I was over everything Peter, I enjoyed watching *Beauty and the Beast* for a few days, then quickly moved on to *Alice in Wonderland*, *The Little Mermaid*, and *The Black Cauldron*, which was kinda weird.

Yesterday, I curled up under my blanket and put on *Mary Poppins* with Julie Andrews and Dick Van Dyke. That was a good one, but when the app suggested that, if I like *Mary Poppins*, I'd like *Bedknobs and Broomsticks*, I decided to throw that one on tonight.

It was good, but sometime around Portobello Road, I was ready to go to bed. Yawning, I click off the downstairs television, turn off the lights, and head upstairs.

But just because I was ready to cozy up in my bed, it didn't mean I was going straight to sleep. I have a full stack of books on the shelf next to my headboard, each one in a varying state of being read. Since it's October, I went all in on my spooky season reads. I'm halfway done with a witch romcom that's as spicy as it is adorable, and that's the one I reach for tonight.

I'm still a couple of chapters away from the climax —though the hero and heroine have *climaxed* a few times already—when I slip my bookmark back into place, then trade the book for my remote.

I can't fall asleep when it's quiet. This is where my sleepy-time show comes into play. I need the sound of the television running, but it can't be something I'm not innately familiar with otherwise I'll stay up to watch it.

Tonight's another *Peter Pan* night, courtesy of the ancient DVD player I keep connected to the even more ancient TV in my bedroom. Knowing me, I'll conk out before he goes searching for his shadow... except, right around the time that Mr. Darling is being a dickhead to Nana, my dozing brain suddenly wakes up as I ask myself: *did you lock the door?*

I want to say that I did. I distinctly remember telling myself that I needed to... but do you think I went through with it? I... I can't recall.

Shit.

There goes any hope of falling right asleep. If I don't go downstairs and double-check, I'll just lie in my bed and convince myself that I didn't... and that I basically hung an **OPEN** sign on my front door for any prospective burglars.

I can't stop thinking about it. I won't, either. And though I'm cozy and would much rather stay under my covers, I scowl and toss them away from me.

Slipping my feet back into my slippers, I huff as I start for the stairs. Real quick, I tell myself. I'll just go double-check the door, call myself an idiot whether it's locked or not, then be back in bed before Wendy and the boys are in Neverland.

Out of habit, I turn on the light switch when I reach the downstairs. The brightness makes me wince, but I shuffle across the floor quickly.

An even quicker tug on the door reveals that I *did* lock it.

Well, at least I made sure of it.

That done, I have every intention of going back upstairs—until I realize that I'm pretty freaking thirsty. That's what you get when you eat canned soup, I guess. That amount of sodium is a killer.

Water. I'll get a glass of water from the kitchen, pee

again before I go back to my room, and then I'll finally
—*finally*—go to sleep.

And I one hundred percent meant that, too—until
I walk into the kitchen and do a double-take.

What the...

Completely forgetting about my thirst, I blink a
couple of times to make sure that I'm actually seeing
what I *think* I'm seeing. But I am, and when I pick the
heavy, leather-bound book up from the middle of my
kitchen table, I gape at it.

Just in case, I hurriedly turn the pages until I reach
that strange title.

Grimoire du Sombra.

What the hell is it doing here? More importantly...
how did it get here?

The door was locked. I just proved that. And even if
it wasn't, what kind of burglar leaves things behind in a
house that they broke into? Because someone had to
have snagged the book, snuck into my house, and left it
here since *I* definitely didn't.

Not remembering if I locked the door or not is one
thing. There's no way I'd forget about stealing a book
from work and leaving it on the kitchen table I barely
use these days.

But if I didn't... who did?

THE BOOK IS STILL SITTING ON MY KITCHEN TABLE WHEN I go down for breakfast the next morning.

I really, really hoped it wouldn't be. If it was gone, I could've pretended that finding it there was part of a dream or something.

Of course, in order to dream, I'd have to have been able to fall asleep first, and after I came downstairs and found the book last night, that wasn't happening anytime soon. Not when all I could think about was the old grimoire that I purposely dropped onto the table before I bolted upstairs as though it would disappear once I turned my back on it.

But it didn't, and after I brew an extra large coffee to get me through the day, I snatch the book, throw it inside my oversized tote so that no one knows I have it, then head off for work.

I hate being late. It's one of my biggest pet peeves, but I lost track of time when I came downstairs and had to face the fact that the book was still in my house. By the time I'm heading out—and after I make sure I lock my house up again—I kick past the new pile of acorns and half-walk, half-jog to the library, knowing that I'll be walking in three minutes past the start of shift.

Thankfully, Moira's not standing near the counter, ready to chew me out. So far, it's only Jake, and he's just putting his phone away when I rush in, the heavy tote banging my hip.

"Hey," I say, moving around him so that I can sign into the computer.

"Hey," he says back. He's holding a coffee of his own, fresh from Dunkin', and he uses it to salute me. "Looks like we're working together again."

Obviously.

I give him a small, tight-lipped smile before I yank the heavy book out of my bag with him watching.

Maybe he didn't notice...

"What's that you got there?"

I don't like to lie; it's up there with being late. However, since I can't really explain *why* I have this book, I decide to come up with an alternate version of the truth for Jake.

Tapping the cover, I tell him, "Someone dropped it in the depository yesterday. I shelved it, but I found it sitting on top of one of the leaf piles under the front window. Weird, huh?"

Taking the book from me, Jake scans the library tag I printed out for it yesterday.

"What's even weirder is that no one even checked it out," he tells me after peering at the computer screen.

I didn't think they would. "Huh. I wonder how it got out of the library."

Jake shrugs, dropping the book onto the rolling cart we use for go-backs. "I don't know, but that reminds me. Did you see there was another break-in last night?"

Yeah, I think to myself. If not the library—which at least has some kind of security system—then someone got into my house last night.

Why? No clue.

Who? I haven't the foggiest idea.

But at least I brought the book back. Jake took it from me, and now that it's out of my hands, I'd like to forget about it as quickly as I can...

Talking about the constant burglaries isn't the best choice for a change of subject, but I can't say that it doesn't serve as one hell of a distraction for me.

I shake my head. "No, sorry. I didn't get the chance to check my phone this morning."

Oh, no. I was too busy obsessing over that strange book, wasn't I?

"I didn't really see it myself, either," Jake says, "but my mom told me as we were both getting ready to leave for work. It was on the early morning show. New York's talking about the break-ins now, too."

That's right. I forgot that Jake lives with his parents. He mentioned that the first time he asked me out on a date *date*, saying something along the lines that—if I wanted—we could hang out at my place because at least there we could have some 'privacy'.

I nipped that shit in the bud real quick. Jake's definitely the Netflix and chill-type, and while I might've accepted what he was so plainly offering if we weren't co-workers, I told him then that, if I wanted to invite him over, I would. And that was that.

Until now, it seems.

"I was thinking, Hope... I know you walk home when work's over. With this guy around, maybe it's not the smartest idea. If you want a ride sometime or... I don't know... to hang out after work, just let me know. I'm usually free."

I'll give him points for perseverance. Jake stays just on the right side of it not being quite sexual harassment, and as nice as his offer is, it's pointless. If I wanted a ride, I could just take my car and he knows that. Then again... after how weird last night was, maybe it won't be a bad idea to have a guy around.

Or maybe I really am just going nuts.

"Sounds nice," I tell him. "I'll let you know when I am."

Maybe.

We'll see.

I THINK I MIGHT HAVE OVERDONE IT ON THE COFFEE.

During my lunch break, I took a page out of Jake's book and had myself a quick stroll on over to Dunkin'. I thought a pumpkin spice latte would help me shake off my sleepless night, but between the caffeine and the sugar—the bavarian cream donut I had for lunch didn't help, either—I'm feeling pretty jittery by the time it's four o'clock and I get to go home.

I'm not ready to take Jake up on his offer of a ride just yet, so I slip out of the library before he can catch up to me—but not before I take a quick stop over to the occult section to make sure that the grimoire is still there.

For probably the twentieth time today I checked, and it's still on the shelf, freaking *taunting* me.

At least I have some peace of mind that I left it behind. I might be sleep-deprived and over-caffeinated and secretly wondering who could possibly be screwing with me like this, but I'm feeling much better as I let myself into my house.

Until I take three steps inside and see the *Grimoire du Sombra* dropped in the middle of my living room, that is.

That's when I start to shriek.

CHAPTER 4
WAIT

SAMMAEL

It took me four cycles of the human moon to find the grimoire.

Four cycles where I've done nothing but watch over my mate, a silent spectator, and search for that damned book whenever I brought myself to leave her side all so that I could find a way to be a demon again, not a phantom.

I put all of my faith in the spellbook. The matefinder incantation made me like this because I didn't wait for my female to summon me; I pray to the gods that it will fix me.

There was one benefit to the cast. After promising myself to my mate—though she does not know it—I formed a whisper-thin bond with her the same time as I lost so much of myself.

It's something small, but I treasure it all the same.

It could've been worse. Unlike Loki, when my spell failed, I didn't turn fully demonic. I still have my essence, though without the ability to touch my mate, I cannot share it with her. I cannot accept hers, either, which means that—when I first appeared in her quarters—I knew nothing about her except that she is a human beauty, and she is mine.

Before I was a mage and part of Duke Haures's guard, I was a student. If I could not rely on her essence to discover who my mate is, I would do it myself. Study... learn... I am determined to know as much as my fated mate as possible and, in the four cycles since I left Sombra, unable to return, I've learned quite a lot.

Her name is Hope. She is a mature female, though I know she hasn't seen as many centuries as I have, and yet... that is part of her charm. In so many ways, she is an innocent, finding wonder all around her.

I adore it.

She spends many of her days in something called a 'library', which reminds me of the archives at the School of Mages. Her specialty is bound books, and I am pleased to see that we both share a fondness for the printed word when I drift through the door of her quarters, following her to her 'job'.

As a Sombra demon—whether in my shadows or my skin—I couldn't pass through structures before now. When I was in my faded shadow form, I could slip through any open gap, but there must be a gap. As a phantom, there is no limitation to where I can go. Still, that doesn't mean much when no one in this realm can see me or hear me, but it made my search for the grimoire a little easier since I didn't have to worry about breaking Duke Haures's first law.

Of course, I had an unfamiliar world to search for the grimoire I lost when the matefinder spell brought me to Hope. None of the mortals would know I was among them, but that did not make it so simple to locate the Sombran spellbook while also watching over my mate, keeping her safe from any harm that might befall her.

My Hope is gentle. She is kind. She is also lonely in a way that I recognize. After all, I was, too, and though my loneliness led me to risk everything to find her, I'd sacrifice even more if it meant I could soothe her lonely heart.

Sometimes, when she glances behind her as though she caught sight of me out of her dull yet lovely human eyes, I wonder if she can see me. If she can *sense* me. I try my best to catch her attention. At first, nothing worked. But about a cycle after I first found her, I discovered that—as a phantom—if I used some of my essence as a replacement for my missing magic, I could touch things.

Not Hope, which was a disappointment, but if I concentrated enough, I could maneuver items that *she* had previously had contact with.

It's because we're partially bonded. I gave her the mating promise when I read the manifestation spell, triggering a tie between us that I pray to the gods she feels even a little.

The more time I spend around her, the stronger it affects me.

The more I get to learn her—to *love* her—the closer I feel to my sweet mortal.

When she sits in front of the rectangle with the moving pictures, I hover behind her, seeing what it is that she likes. Slowly, over the last four cycles, I've begun to understand some of her human language. With that, I also find ways to show her that I am here. That I already consider her to be my mate.

And I do my best to show her that.

My Hope tends to misplace some of her trinkets. Once I've seen where she keeps them, I try to move them back. Those jingling bits of metal belong on the hook by the door to her home, while her favored foot coverings must stay together. And the 'mote' she's always searching for... to see her smile when she finds it on the edge of her chair where I placed it for her makes my chest swell with pride.

If only it had been as simple for me to find the *Grimoire du Sombra*...

In between my fevered searches for the book, I devoted all of my attention to trying to reach Hope any way I could. And after I watched one of her 'movies' with her, learning exactly what a 'kiss' is... I do just that.

I'd heard the human word before from Susanna, Duke Haures's formerly mortal mate. Though she knows Sombran as well as any demon in our realm, because of the essence exchange, the duke also understands the human tongue. In Mavro, Susanna is the only human mate. Because of that, when she wants to say something to Duke Haures without any of his subjects knowing, she would slip into the human tongue instead.

She would often ask Duke Haures for a 'kiss', but because he would leave the throne room and join his mate in the garden oasis in the center of the capital to give her one, I never knew what exactly it was.

Until I saw from Hope's 'movie' about a flying human child that a 'kiss' is one of those small nuts that fall from those verdant trees so different from the ash trees back in Sombra.

Humans are odd creatures. They must be to find pleasure in such a small nut—or why else would Susanna demand them from her male—but if Duke

Haures pleases his mate by giving her a 'kiss', I will give my beloved Hope hundreds.

I spend hours gathering 'kisses' for Hope every evening, when the shadows fall and the brightness of the human sun doesn't weaken me. I can only use my essence to move those that she's stepped on as she leaves her quarters, but while I can pass through her door, the acorns cannot. So I leave them just outside, waiting for her to see them and know that it's a sign of affection from her male.

And when that's done, I follow any trace of Sombra in the human world I can find to continue to search for the grimoire.

There are two bonded pairs who live in the human realm. Neither Nox and his mate nor Malphas and his sense me when I follow my instincts to their villages, but once I realized that they were the source of demonkind I sensed, I kept searching.

And then, two nights ago, I finally found it.

I worried that I wouldn't be able to bring it back to Hope. Luckily, because it is still part of Sombra—part of *me*—when I pick it up, the grimoire becomes as transparent and insubstantial as I am as a phantom. It also solidifies when I drop it, as I know because it did when I put it in the drawer at Hope's 'library'.

I wanted her to have it find her the same way that the charm led the grimoire to fall into the other human females' claw-free hands. I rushed our mating by reading the spell instead of her, and I presented the book to her at her 'work' so that it could imprint on her now.

But, when it did, Hope didn't recognize that the grimoire was fated to belong to her. After flipping through it, ignoring the true love spell inside, she put it with all the other bound books in her 'library'.

Watching her from the shadows, I took the book back, bringing it to her home.

Unlike the 'kisses', I could carry the grimoire inside, placing it on the table that Hope often uses. She didn't seem pleased that I returned it to her, though after I retrieved it again and again—not quite understanding why she would shout that one time when she saw that I had—she finally accepted that it belonged with her.

At least, she didn't try to carry it back to her 'library' again. However, my mate refused to open it, no matter how often I moved it within her reach while she was distracted by the talking rectangle on her wall, and I had to come up with another way to get her to understand.

I need her to read the true love spell. It seems like the only way I can return to a solid form would be if Hope summons me to her, but without getting her to understand that that's what she must do, I'm stuck.

When all my essence is crying out to be given to

her, it's torture—but it's no more than I deserve for my impatience.

Loving your mate is instinctive for every Sombra demon. Our gods grant us only one, and they're never, ever wrong. When we find our mate, we don't hesitate.

Humans are different. I've learned much of their strange customs since I've been trapped in their world, and reactions that perplexed me at the time make more sense now that I have a human female of my own.

I never could understand why Malphas's pale-haired female made him wait until the night of the gold moon and he was about to be dragged in chains back to Sombra before she claimed him in return. If she was his mate, wouldn't she have wanted to bond herself to him immediately?

I had thought so—but I've now known of my beloved for four cycles and I'm no closer to claiming my forever mate than I was when I was a full-blooded demon in Sombra, serving under the duke.

My heart beats for her. Every breath I take is for Hope. I become part of the human world, try to learn their tongue, and I do it all for her.

The bond is there. I can follow it to her, no matter where she goes, though I do try to give her her privacy. It's not right to see that which isn't mine quite yet, so I always stand guard outside of the small room where she keeps her toilet and her shower stall. I will see her naked form when she allows me to, no sooner, though when it comes to her pleasure…

I am a weak male. When she finds her pleasure with the false cock that hums and buzzes, I hunger to watch her, but dutifully close my eyes to it before drifting from her private quarters to the floor below. As a phantom, my senses are duller than they were when I was a demon, but I would have to slice off my nose and my ears not to smell her delicious musk and hear her soft, whimpering cries.

One day, they will be for me.

Until then, I do my best to come up with a way so I can reveal myself to her. It's been seven human days—marked by every time Hope slumbers during the time of shadows—since I first brought the grimoire to her, and she's kept it tucked away beneath her bedding for safekeeping.

And then, on the cusp of the next earthly cycle of its singular moon, I'm hovering in the corner of her quarters, watching her sleep fitfully when I finally sense something I've longed for for centuries.

My female is tugging on her end of our fated mate bond.

Since I've been broken, shattered, *splintered* into a phantom, I have not been able to summon a portal to return to Sombra. It's as though the human world is keeping me here until I can either release my tie to Hope—or convince her to accept it.

I never attempted to use a portal to travel in search of the spellbook. I only followed the traces of Sombra that lingered in this realm, but when I think back on how far of a distance I was able to travel, maybe I did subconsciously summon one.

A Sombra mage, portals have always been one of my specialties. I could cross over countless planes, including the human world, Sombra, Soleil, and more... including the dream plane.

I've been there once before, helping Duke Haures reach his human mate when Bazael tried to harm her. I had forgotten about it, but when I sense the tug and see the hazy patch of opalescent-like shadow hovering around the level of my horns, I'm suddenly reminded.

That's when I understand just *where* my Hope is calling me to her. As though part of her has finally accepted that I am here, that I would do anything for her, and that I have enough magic stored deep inside of me to reach her after all... when she tugs on our bond, I'm helpless but to answer her, touching the shimmering ball with my claw and allowing it to carry me to her.

After all, she is my mate. There is nothing in this world or any other that would prevent me from going to her when she calls.

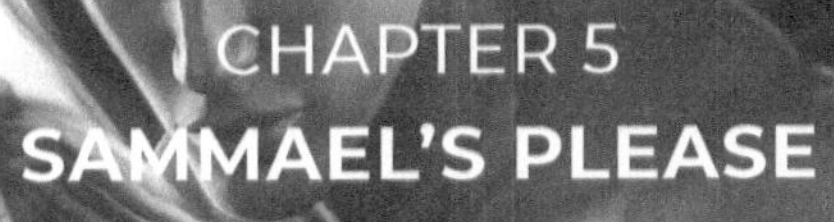

CHAPTER 5
SAMMAEL'S PLEASE

HOPE

I've always been a very vivid dreamer.

Growing up, there were times that I would wake up, convinced something had happened, only to have Johanna tease me that I was seeing things while I slept again.

What can I say? If I wasn't a librarian, maybe I would've been a storyteller. I love reading, love watching movies, and if my grammar was better, who knows? Maybe I would've become a creative instead of happily settling down to be a guardian of books.

Nowadays, I get most of my creative outlet in my dreams; and not only nowadays, either. From as far back as I can recall, I would often have a faceless, featureless shadow creature that would visit me there.

59

He—because I was sure it was a *he*—never spoke, and he always lurked far away, melding into the other shadows, but I wasn't afraid.

Shocking, huh? I'm scared of nearly everything else, but a shadow creature?

Oh, no. Why would *that* frighten me?

You think he would. Nope. As a kid, I thought of him as a guardian angel. As an adult, I rarely thought of him as all.

Lately, though, I've had a few dreams where it seems like I'm the one searching for him. As a vivid dreamer, I can't really tell if I'm asleep or not, and I seem to control the narrative, trying to trigger a story in my head while watching to see how it would play out.

That's what happens tonight.

In my dream, I'm still in my room. Instead of wearing the PJs I fell asleep in, I've got on a pretty white nightgown that the real Hope would *never* wear. I'm not lying in my bed, but sitting cross-legged at the foot of it, staring at my closed door, willing it open.

It doesn't—but that doesn't mean that *nothing* happens.

As I watch curiously, the shadows in the far corner of my bedroom start to thicken. Dream Hope gasps. I remember… whenever the shadow creature came to watch me, that's how he would arrive. In a mass of shadows before he separated himself from them.

Just like he does now.

Only... once the shadow monster, with his dual horns rising above his dark head, wafts away from the corner, drifting so that he's only about five feet away from the foot of my bed, he *shifts*.

He changes.

He's... well, he's still a monster. But, suddenly, I can see what those shadows have long hidden.

So tall that the tips of his shiny, black horns are scraping my ceiling when he pulls himself up to his full height, he's twice as wide as I am, with skin the color of a Red Delicious apple. He has thick black hair, the same shade as mine, but while my hair just about reaches my chin, his cascades down his back.

And his eyes...

I've never seen his eyes before. I would've remembered if I did. They're big and wide-set, glowing out of his strong features, a brilliant purple color that totally clashes with his skin tone.

They're beautiful. And, though he is the opposite of any human guy I've ever seen, so is he.

Of course he is. I conjured him up in my dreams, even going so far as to make him shirtless so that I can drool over his muscular chest. If I was feeling a little racier, I might've gone for no pants, but his bottom half is still wrapped up in shadows from his waist to his calves. His feet are solid and red, though, and they're standing on my floor as he looks down on me.

His expression is one of surprise. Almost as though it's a shock for him to see me. Is it because I'm a human and probably very small and weak and pale compared to him? Or because this is my dream and that's how I think a strapping monster like this guy would react to being in a room with me?

Who knows? Now that he's here, I'm just hanging on, waiting to see what will happen next.

He opens his mouth, showing off a pair of fangs that would put any neighborhood vampire to shame. In a voice that's not as deep as I would've expected from such a big guy, he says something, but I have no idea what. It's not any language I've ever heard before, and if I thought I picked up 'Hope' somewhere in the middle of that... welp. It's my dream. Why wouldn't he know my name?

I wave at him. "Hi."

He looks at his hand. For a moment, I expect him to mimic my gesture, waving back, but he doesn't. Instead, his face screws up, forming deep lines that rival the strange ridges that are on his forehead.

Then, trailing one pointed claw along the top of his muscular arm, he keeps his eyes locked on me as he says, "*Please.*"

Hang on—

"You know English?"

If I conjured up a monster who knows English, why didn't he say so in the first place?

He frowns again. He lifts his hand, showing me his thumb and his forefinger, careful not to let his claws touch. As he keeps them apart, it's obvious he's showing off the slight gap between them as he rasps out, "Little."

Okay. He knows a little English.

That's okay. I mean, I've gotta be imagining this whole exchange in the first place, but I work at a library in one of the most diverse states in America. The only time Moira doesn't have a conniption when she sees one of us with our phones out is when we're using a translation app to service our patrons.

This is right out of my real life. Looking over at my nightstand, I see my phone where I habitually try to leave it. Getting up and grabbing it, I engage the translator app before moving so that I'm standing right by him.

I point to my mouth, then move my fingers, gesturing for him to speak.

It takes a second before he rattles off something in that same language from before.

Once he's done, I tell the app that I don't know what language it is, assuming that the people who programmed it should.

No dice. The translator app searches and searches and eventually spits out nothing that makes any sense to me.

Man. It would've been so much easier to see why

the monster clearly wants me to touch his arm if he could tell me. I'm pretty sure his 'little' bit of English won't be able to help us out here when it comes to that, and since I'm probably the mastermind behind this and *I* have no idea, it makes sense that he just wants me to do it without any explanation.

It's a dream. What'll really go wrong if I touch the monster in my dream? It's not like he can hurt me. Besides, I can just wake up if this gets too weird.

I gesture at him with my fingers. "Sure. Gimme."

Does he understand that? I guess so because he puts his forearm within my reach.

He's hot—and I don't mean his strong yet surprisingly attractive appearance. My fingertip nearly sizzles when I press it against his strange red skin, though maybe that was just an electric jolt stemming from this weird connection that already seems to exist between us. Following his example, I slide my finger up his arm and back, and while his skin definitely started out way too hot for me, it's just a little bit feverish by the time I'm backing away from him.

As though he doesn't want to lose that connection, he takes two steps after me.

"Hope." My name comes out in a purr, his purple eyes shining brightly. "You honor me with your essence."

See that? That right there puts me firmly in the "you must be dreaming" camp. There was no point in continuing what would inevitably become a monster-fucker fantasy if I couldn't actually communicate with him before I start drooling. I'm a modern woman who enjoys her sexuality, but consent is a biggie for me. Even in my wet dreams, I'm not going to openly lust over the monster of my dreams when he has no idea that that's what I'm doing.

I mean, that's why his bottom half is covered up, after all. If I really want to see what he's hiding, I gotta be able to *ask* him about it.

Still, something's weird about this. And, yeah, something's weird about my lusty brain coming up with a monster in my dreams for me to fantasize over instead of, like, Ryan Gosling or Jason Momoa or some Hollywood hunk... and, true, this guy kinda looks like Jason Momoa if he didn't have tattoos or he was red with purple eyes... but still...

Ignoring the growing lust I feel for my fantasy, I toss my phone to my bed and jab one finger in his direction.

"Hey... I thought you said you can only speak a little English."

"Yes. That is true. From your rectangle with the moving pictures, I've learned some. A little. I'm a very good student." His gorgeous chest puffs out in obvious pride. "I was the top of my class at the School of Mages before I was handpicked to serve under the duke."

I don't really understand a lot of what he said, but

one thing for sure: that's a lot of English right there.

When I point that out, he says, "Now I am fluent. Because of your essence."

"My *what*?"

What is he talking about?

He waves his hand, gesturing at all of me. "Your essence. That which makes Hope *Hope*."

Oh. Like my soul, I guess.

Wait—

"I don't get it."

"It's simple to understand, my mortal mate. With your touch and your open heart, you honored your male with your essence. You gave me everything that you are, and I've accepted it. Now I know everything about you, including your human tongue."

He says 'human' like he's not. 'Mortal', too. And while he's obviously *not* human... what about being mortal?

Who is he?

Who have I created?

"What is your name?"

He raps his chest with his fist. "I am Sammael. Favored mage to Duke Haures, and Hope McReary's male."

Excuse me?

"Sammael." His name is foreign on my tongue. Still, he preens when he hears me say it. "What do you mean, my male?"

"You are my mate."

Yeah... that's still not helping me.

He holds out his hand again. "Touch me more. Touch me while you can. You don't know how I've longed just to feel your soft human fingertips on my skin."

Something about the way he says that has me paying attention to his. Whoa. At the end of every one of his fingers is a pointed, black claw that's at least an inch long—and a lot more intimidating now that I' focusing on them.

Good thing he's not asking to touch *me*. With claws like that, he could rip me to shreds if he wanted to. Not like I get the vibe he would... but this is a dream. Despite how vivid it is, I shouldn't be able to touch him at all. And if I did? Is it normal to be able to sense how warm he is? My fingers still hold his heat... and, even so, I kinda want to touch him again.

I kinda want to do more than that...

Inching toward him, rubbing my thumb against my forefinger even though I know damn well I'm about to stroke his arm again next, I ask, "Are you sure? I mean... nothing's going to happen to me if I do?"

"This is the dream-plane," he says by way of answer. "It is a miracle that I could accept your essence, but maybe that's because you already recognize Sammael as your male."

Or maybe I need to stop watching Halloween movies so late at night.

"Go on, Hope," he murmurs. "Learn your mate. Hold him. And, for this moment in time, allow me to hold you."

I can't tell you the last time someone just wanted to hold me. Not to have sex or to convince me that they'll stop at just a handjob or even a blowie. But hold me like I'm something precious?

Oh, yeah.

This is definitely a dream—but I let him do it, enjoying the feel of his big body as he swoops me up into his embrace, keeping me close...

DREAMS END.

It's the sad fact of life that, one moment, I was clinging to my monster. The next? I'm coming to, alone in my bed, with just the memory of his warmth on my skin.

Only... woof. I *am* warm.

More than warm, actually.

My room is usually kept at a balmy sixty-eight degrees lately since I refuse to turn the heat on when October weather in New Jersey can vary from one extreme to the next, but it doesn't matter. When I wake up the next morning, I'm drenched in sweat.

Like, literally *drenched.*

What the...

My hair is stuck to my face. When I pull myself up, my pajamas are stuck to my skin. Lifting my hand, pressing the back of it to my forehead, then my cheeks, I'm shocked by how hot I feel.

Is that a fever? It feels like a fever. I'm not achy, though, and usually when I'm coming down with something, I get muscle cramps and achy bones.

This is something different.

I don't like it.

Worse, when I force myself to get to my feet, the fabric of my clothing rubs me raw. I have the sudden urge to strip. Figuring that, if I'm naked, I won't be so hot, I tug off my clothes in a frantic rush.

It doesn't help.

It should have, but it doesn't, and now that I'm standing here without any clothes on, I realize just how much my sudden urges have changed. Instead of just stripping, I reach between my legs, cupping my pussy, gasping at the jolt that passes through me the moment I touch my swollen pussy lips.

What the—

Okay. Something's wrong.

Something's wrong, and I don't know what, but now that I'm wide awake, I do what I do in situations where I can't immediately figure out what's going on.

I do my best to ignore it.

CHAPTER 6

THE PERFECT EXCUSE

HOPE

As the day goes on, there's no denying that the fever I woke up with hasn't gone away.

Not even bringing iced coffee to work helped the heat rushing through my veins, and when I popped a few Tylenol, hoping to break it, all that happened was that I got a stomach ache from the medicine.

All in all, I feel like *shit*.

Is this the flu? Something worse?

Am I dying?

I think I'm dying.

I haven't had the actual flu in almost a decade. The last time I had a full-blown case, I was in high school and missed an entire week of midterm assessments.

My fever was so high that everything I saw had an orange tint on it for days, and I think I passed out on the couch at my mom's house for almost a week.

But this? This is something different. Something *weird*. Though I'm not sure what this is, I don't think it's the flu.

Why?

No matter how many years it's been, I'd remember if it made me *this* horny.

Shit. I don't know what kind of illness makes me feel like, if I got laid, I'd feel a hundred times better. My tits are heavy and achy. My poor pussy is slick and hot; I'm so wet that it's leaving splotches on my panties. I brought my vibe in the shower with me, grateful I splurged for the waterproof one, but despite coming *twice* beneath the cool spray, I'm even hotter when I'm done.

And I mean that *both* ways: my temperature, and my need to go find a guy and bang it out.

But since I can't tell Moira I'm calling out with these symptoms, I suck it up and head out to the library, hoping that spending eight hours at work will be enough to distract me from this weirdo illness.

It doesn't.

I do my best to hide it. I offer to cull some of the least-visited shelves so that I can be by myself, and if anyone notices my frequent trips to the bathroom, they're polite enough not to mention it. Too bad the cramps only get worse as the day goes on. My stomach is tight, the back of my neck slick with sweat. At one point, my breath gets shallow and I don't even notice it until I'm panting like a freaking porn star, only without the dick to get me off.

Clamping my mouth shut, hoping no one heard me, my sudden embarrassment that I let this overwhelming need get to me is enough to help me through the next part of my shift.

For most of it, I did manage to avoid anyone else. When it's time to sign out and get ready to go home?

That's when things get a little dicey.

Jake was working the counter most of our shift. It's been a couple of days since our schedules coincided—Jake was off the last two, with me having one of my off days on Monday—and I smiled at him this morning before quickly making myself scarce.

I had hoped to avoid him on my way out like I have been lately, but as though fate is conspiring against me along with this inexplicable illness, he's standing in front of the computer when I go to sign out.

Does Jake always smell so freaking delicious? I don't usually stand too close to him, but I was so eager to just log out that I sidled up to him without waiting for him to scoot over so that I could reach the keyboard.

That was my mistake. Breathing in his scent—a mixture of soap and the rich cologne he wears sparingly but really stands out today—I gasp and, without even realizing I've done it, inch closer to him.

For a moment, Jake's expression is one of surprise, yet delight, almost like he's been waiting to be this close to me without pushing himself on me. But then, as though noticing there's obviously something off about me, he frowns.

"Are you feeling okay? You look a little flushed."

That's better than me wondering if he'd be up for a quickie in the library bathroom... but I am.

I totally am.

That should've been my first real clue that something was more wrong than I initially thought. Before, I just about convinced myself that I was dying. As Jake moves into me, concern written on his adorable face while his cologne continues to go straight to my head... and my vagina... I ask myself: why was I so against getting to know him? Sure, he's my co-worker, but what if I'm giving up on a good thing because I'm too worried about things getting awkward at work if it all goes south?

"I'm fine," I lie. Then again, if he really meant it when he said we could go out... get to know each other... maybe end up somewhere private... I just might be. "I was feeling a little weird earlier, but I'm okay. I think I just need to eat something."

I need more than that, but maybe food will help first.

Fingers crossed.

I guess I know Jake better than I thought because, right on cue, he offers. "I was thinking about going to the Westfield Diner for a quick dinner after work. They have the best reuben sandwiches around... you want to come with?"

He has invited me out at least ten times since he started at the library at the beginning of the summer. Each time, I turn him down.

Today?

My eyes might be glazed over, and the fever is making it so that my freaking clit is pulsing in time to the beat of my frantic heart, but that doesn't stop me from saying, "You know what? Yeah. I'd like that."

And if dinner leads to something that might help me shake off this lust... I'd like that, too.

I KEEP THINKING THAT I'LL WIMP OUT. THAT, BY THE time dinner is done and Jake offers to drive me home, I'll stop listening to my hormones and figure out another way to get past this weirdo sickness.

At one point, when Jake excuses himself between his sandwich and the slice of pumpkin pie he ordered for us to share, I pull out my phone. First, I use my reverse camera to make sure that I don't look as much of a sweaty, hot mess as I feel; surprisingly, apart from the way my pupils seem larger than normal, I look alright. That bit of a vanity check done, I hurriedly open up Google.

I tried my best to look up my symptoms this morning before I left for the library, but since they've only gotten worse as the day's gone by, I decide to see if another search might unlock some secret illness that I've never heard of before.

If only. Everything I find on WebMD only reaffirms my fear that I'm either dying or going through super early perimenopause and this fever is really hot flashes. My desire to go to bed with anyone who might be interested? That's common for some women. With their hormones in flux, their libido gets out of control. As a heterosexual female, anyone with a dick starts to look good.

And Jake... he's looking *real* good.

Over dinner, I discover we have more in common than just a fondness for Whiskey Rose and a tendency to doomscroll when it comes to the news. Like me, he's a younger sibling; also like me, he grew up on Disney, though he hasn't watched any of their movies in years.

He remembered that Captain Hook is the villain of Peter Pan, though. And he teasingly asked me, if I wanted to fly, what my happy thoughts would be.

Okay. He's flirting. I expected that, and when he scoops up a piece of his pie on his fork before offering it to me, there's no denying that he considers this some kind of date. I'm not doing anything to make him think differently. In fact, when I tap his shoe with my sneaker beneath the table before taking that bite, I'm kinda flirting back a little.

Around the time the waitress stops by the table to see if we want coffee before we go, I've put a stop to it. I shake my head to coffee—and another bite from his fork when mine works just as well—but that's only because, out of nowhere, I get that feeling like I'm being watched again.

How nice. Now I'm still horny as hell, plus I can't ignore the sensation that someone other than just Jake is paying close attention to the way I'm wiggling in my seat.

So I decline the coffee. Jake does, too, and as the waitress walks away to get our check—that I already told him I'm going dutch on for reasons I can't even explain to myself right now—he says, "You usually bring coffee from home to work. I thought... when we're done here, maybe we can have a cup back at your place."

If I had any doubt that he's hoping the night would end the same way I am, it's gone now. A guy in his early twenties, I'm not surprised that he'll take any chance to get laid.

As for me... if I invite him in for a nightcap, whether it's coffee, tea, or some wine, I'm going to sleep with him.

Am I using him? I don't want to think that I am. He's cute, he's nice, he's caring... and when I insisted on going dutch, he argued briefly before accepting that I wasn't about to budge. He wants sex. *I* want sex. We're both consensual adults... and tomorrow is another day.

I'll deal with it when it comes.

But tonight? As he pulls up outside of my house, I tell him where he can park so that we can go inside for a cup of coffee together.

It seemed like a good idea all the way up until I'm standing on the porch, anxiously knocking aside the most recent pile of acorns left in front of my door. By the time I'm unlocking it, Jake's hand ghosting over the small of my back, I already know I'm making a huge mistake.

It only gets worse as he looks around my house in wonder as I flip on the lights.

"This is nice, Hope. Real nice." He pauses for a moment before his lips quirk upward slightly. "I bet the rest of the house is nice, too. The kitchen... the bathrooms... the bedrooms."

Oh, boy. "Yup. It's a rental, but I've been here a couple of years now. I've really had a chance to make it my own."

"I'm hoping to move out of my parents' place soon. You'll have to give me some tips."

As long as he doesn't think I'm looking for a roommate or anything, sure. "Of course. But, um, why don't you sit down? I'll go get the coffee."

"Sure—"

Crash.

Jake was just starting for my couch when something clattering against my hardwood floor has both of us looking around.

That's when I see my remote on the ground. Weird. It's something I lose so freaking often that I try to make a conscious effort to return it to its place on the couch's armrest. I'm pretty sure that was where it was two seconds ago, but somehow it slipped off of the couch and crashed to the floor.

Luckily, the back didn't pop off. That happens pretty frequently, too, especially when I absently knock into it, sending it flying. I've lost more batteries that way, the small cylinders rolling out of sight and out of mind.

Picking the remote up, I show it off to Jake, then toss it onto the couch. "Now, about that coffee... how would you like it?"

"However you take yours is fine."

I nod, then tell him I'll be right back.

The entire time I'm getting two mugs of coffee ready, I'm having second thoughts. It was one thing to fantasize about my co-worker earlier because he was the only guy around. Now that I'm home... I don't know. I'm not as horny as I was, though I am still feeling sick.

During dinner at the diner, he leaned across the table and placed the back of his hand against my forehead. I hadn't expected it, and when I felt his clammy touch against my overheated skin, it was all I could do to keep my food down.

When I think about letting Jake touch me now... I'm back to being nauseous.

Maybe the coffee will help, I decide. Grabbing the two mugs, I head back to the living room, jolting a little when one of the pictures of me and the twins happens to fall backward on its shelf as I pass it.

What the—

Ignoring it, I go over to where Jake's waiting for me on the couch. I give him his mug, then keep mine between both of my hands. Compared to my feverish skin, it's barely warm, and as much as I try to force myself to, I can't compel my hands to bring it to my lips.

Jake doesn't seem too interested in the contents of his mug, either. Setting it down on the slightly lopsided coffee table in front of my couch, he turns to look at me.

"Hope," he murmurs, inching his face closer to me.

Shit. He's going to kiss me, isn't he?

I swallow, frantically trying to figure out how to

avoid his kiss without offending him—or him rightfully accusing me of leading him on.

And that's when my front door suddenly slams wide open, scaring the crap out of me... while also giving me the perfect excuse to get up and dash away from Jake.

CHAPTER 7
KISS

SAMMAEL

My Hope is being lusted after by another male.

He is fortunate that my magic still has yet to return to me. I'd use every one of the secret spells that us mages pass among each other when we're still students to zap him.

There's one I heard of that makes a demon lose one of his horns. If I could cast it on the human, maybe his cock will fall off. I'd like to see him try to mate my Hope without it.

Obviously, that isn't possible now. There is no way for me to confront the male, or to show myself to Hope while she is awake. Not when I'm still a phantom.

Part of me had believed that, when she was conscious again, she'd still think fondly of the male she met in her dreams. After she gave me her essence with a simple brush of her finger, I could finally communicate with her. I know her tongue as if it is my own.

And I know that this male is asking things of her that should be reserved for Hope's true mate.

Me.

The most I can do in this state is try to catch her attention by moving some of the objects in her home. I knock her 'mote'—the control for her rectangle... ah, her *television remote*—to the ground.

With a confused expression, she picks it up and places it back on the edge of her furniture.

Something more noticeable, then.

There isn't anything that Hope has not touched in her quarters. As she brings two steaming mugs from the kitchen, I use the tip of my claw to send a picture of Hope with two younger spawn—her kin—tumbling to its back.

She frowns, but doesn't stop to fix it. Instead, she joins the male on the couch, offering him one of the drinks.

He sets it down on the small table in front of them before sidling closer to my Hope.

Fury and jealousy rushing through me, I use as

much of my gathered energy as I can to force the doorway to her home to push inward, leaving a path for the male to take.

"Out," I grumble, knowing full well that neither can hear me. "Go."

It is my beloved mate who rises up from her couch first. Rushing over to the open door, she pauses with one hand on the knob.

With the other, Hope cradles her belly.

She is not with spawn. Since the matefinder spell tied us together, she has not mated any other male, though this human thinks that she will choose him tonight. From her essence, I also know that my beloved mate is not interested in having offspring with any male. Her kin already does, and while Hope loves those wee humans, she would be content to never have any of her own.

Since I feel the same, that just goes to show that the gods have chosen the perfect mate for me—and, yet, this human male thinks he can have her...

No.

He gets to his feet, frowning at the open door. "Are you okay?"

"Um. Yeah. Must've just been the wind," she begins before shaking her head quickly, her pretty dark hair hitting her chin as it sways. "Actually, no. I'm sorry, Jake. I thought the coffee might settle my stomach but... I think you were right. I'm not feeling so great right now."

"I told you your forehead was hot."

She gulps. "I know. I'm pretty sure I'm feverish. I definitely think I'm coming down with something. I don't want you to get sick."

Fever... sick...

Oh. Oh my gods.

No.

Hope might be sick. It's not a fever, though. At least, not one that a human would normally have.

But a mate? One that triggered the essence exchange but didn't follow through with the mating promise or taking her male's seed, finalizing their bond?

It doesn't happen all that often. In Sombra, when a demon finds his mate, he usually has her bonded to him that very same eve. The gold moon deadline is only imposed by Duke Haures when the mate is human because of his first law. A demon and his demoness can form their bond whenever they wish, though they very rarely wait.

And if, for some reason, they do? Our instincts are wired to push us toward our one true mate.

I would make Hope mine now if I could. The gods won't punish me for rejecting the gift they so graciously gave me.

But my mate... I told her last night that she was

mine. I asked her to touch me and she did, giving me her essence at the same time, but it was in the dream plane. I never thought that would be enough to begin the mating dance between us.

Obviously, I was wrong.

There is only one cure for the mating sickness: *mating*. To ward the symptoms off for a while, an intimate touch from her male should be enough to keep her from feeling the overwhelming heat and need that comes with the fever.

But I cannot touch her. At least, not until she falls asleep and dreams.

Thankfully, Hope does not turn to this human male to ease her need. After telling him that she is sick, she uses the open door to gesture that he should go. The male—this Jake—tries to get her to agree that he should stay, but my Hope is firm. They will talk again when she's feeling better. Until then, he must leave.

With a regrettable expression, he does.

I grin. I probably should not, not when my Hope is suffering so. I cannot help it. From her essence, I know that I am not the first male she has been intimate with. That doesn't bother me. She didn't know of Sammael then, so why would she wait for a mate who might never find her? She is human, not Sombran, and that is how some humans search for their life partners.

There is no magic in this realm. Not like how I was led to believe before I spent more than four cycles here. The humans fated to find a Sombra demon mate are touched by something that none of the other mortals share, and they can only master the *verus amor* spell because the gods gave them the power to find their forever.

Just like they gave my Hope the ability to call me to her on the dream-plane.

I hope she will tonight. Her body craves something only I can provide. Because, while the human male might have been able to touch her intimately if she allowed it, he is not her fated mate. His touch would not ease her mate sickness.

Mine will, and if she calls to me, I will be there to do anything she asks of me to make her feel better.

In the dream-plane, I can be whole.

I can be aroused.

If she asks it of me, I can mate her.

And I will.

For Hope, I will do *anything*.

I HOVER CLOSE BEHIND HOPE FOR THE REST OF THE night.

I cannot touch her. I still have faith that simply being near her might be enough to help her with the worst of the mate sickness. And maybe it does because, after she finishes her drink, she's able to eat a little food before she goes upstairs to rest.

She must feel terrible. Rather than grab one of her small books to read before she turns on the rectangle with the moving pictures, she shucks her clothes—I give her my back as she does—then climbs in among her bedding.

She's snoring softly before I know it. Sucking in a breath that isn't necessary in this half-life of mine, I wait to see if she'll tug on the growing bond between us.

When she does, I quickly answer.

Arriving on the dream-plane, I immediately take the chance to revert to my demon shape again. She seemed to like it the last time we met, and while I often spend most of my time in my shadows, this is the true me. I want my mate to be attracted to my healthy red skin and shiny onyx horns.

From the scent of her musk perfuming the dream-plane, it's easy to tell that she is *definitely* attracted to something.

As I appear, she immediately rises up from her bedding. She had been lying down, covered, but as she shifts, the covering falls, revealing her breasts to me.

"Oh," she says, her voice throaty. "It's you again."

My body immediately comes to life. Thankfully, I conjured shadows to shield my lower half otherwise my mate would be greeted by an impressive cockstand.

I am constantly aroused by my Hope. As a phantom, my body does not react; as a demon, it is all I can do not to take my cock in hand, finding momentary relief. But if I ache to mate her, I can only imagine how she feels after suffering from mate sickness since this morning.

My tongue darts out. I lick my lips, then croak out, "It is I, my mate. And you... you have bared yourself to me."

She glances down as though she had no idea her breasts were out. Shrugging, they bounce as she leaves them free. "They're just tits. I'm sure you've seen plenty before."

I... have not. I know there are some Sombrans who settle for any demoness because they are randy and lonely—especially some students in the School of Mages—but I was not one of them. I have never seen a naked female as a mature male until Hope blessed me with this vision.

And when she mutters something about it being 'hellish hot in here' before throwing the last of her coverings away, I get my first full sight of her cunt.

I don't know if demonesses in Sombra have a patch of hair protecting their cunt like my Hope does. Sombran demons do not, but most demonesses are from Soleil, a neighboring plane. They have horns and a deep golden shade to their skin, with smaller breasts and wider hips than my Hope... and that is all I know.

It matters not. This is the female given to me, and she is perfect in every way.

And I am all the more grateful for my coverings so that I do not frighten her with how desperately I want her.

In the dream-plane, I am alive in every way. My nose scents how much her body is begging to be touched, and my ears pick up on her heaving breaths. My body is tight and hot and heavy. My claws itch to touch her soft skin again... and, with the mate sickness affecting her, I see no reason why I shouldn't.

"It is hot," I agree, "but that is because you are sick."

"You're telling me."

I am telling her. "It is the mate sickness," I say. "Your body is in need—"

Under her breath, barely listening to me, Hope mutters, "Trust me, I know what it needs. That's why I invited Jake over."

Jake. The other male.

Swallowing my jealousy, I move toward her. When she doesn't shift away from me, I ease down onto her bedding with her.

"Take my hand. This should help."

To my surprise, Hope doesn't even hesitate. Snatching my hand, she clings to me, sighing in relief the moment our skin touches.

"Yes," she murmurs. "Holy shit. That's so much better."

"I thought it might help. Though, if you'll allow it, a more... intimate touch should ease you even further."

"Intimate?" she echoes. "You know... let's just do this for now."

Of course. "Anything for you, my mate."

"You keep calling me that," she says after a moment. "Last night, too. What... when you say 'mate', what do you mean?"

Ah. I have her essence, but she doesn't have mine. So she doesn't know...

"Mate. My..." I search her essence for the proper word. "My wife."

Her eyelids flutter as she makes a harsh noise in her throat. "I'm sorry. *What*?"

Was that the wrong word? "What do you call a partner that one mates with, procreates with, and loves with all their heart? So much so that they choose to be together for the rest of their existence?"

"Uh." Hope exhales, but she doesn't release my hand just yet. "I guess 'wife' works, but why do you think *I* am your, er, mate?"

"Because the gods gave you to me. You were fated to be mine."

"How do you know that?"

I gesture at our intertwined hands, her small white fingers nearly lost in my much larger red ones.

"Because, if you were not, my touch would not ease your mate sickness."

Before, when I told her it was the mate sickness, I don't think she was paying attention. This time? She does—and she immediately drops my hand.

"Did you do this to me? Make me sick like this?"

There is no denying that this is my fault. "I'm so sorry, my mate—"

"Mate," she says weakly.

"—but I never intended to make you ill. I vow it."

She glances up at me, her pretty blue eyes so dull, yet so charming. "Wow. I... I actually believe you. Whatever you did to me sucked, but you... you wouldn't hurt me. I really do believe that."

I am glad she does. From our bond, I can sense that she means everything she said... but I can also tell that my Hope is struggling to understand just what it means to be my mate.

If only she were a demoness from Soleil. I wouldn't have to explain mate bonds and forever... but if she *were* a demoness from Soleil, she wouldn't be my Hope.

I never want her to doubt me. All I want is to show her that I am the proper male for her and I think I am failing.

"I wish I could give you a 'kiss'," I tell her mournfully. "Maybe then you would know how much I care for you."

I leave all of my 'kisses' outside because I have not found a way to carry one inside for my Hope. Because of that, I have none to offer her here on this dream-plane.

She had dropped her gaze to our hands. At my wistful comment, her head snaps up. "Excuse me?"

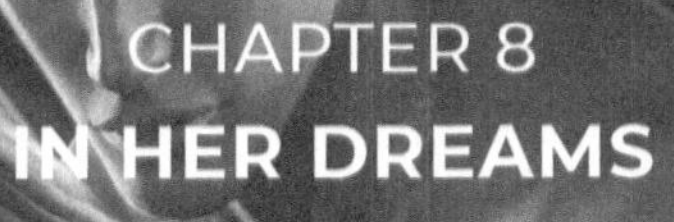

SAMMAEL

"A 'kiss'," I say again, in case she didn't hear me. "Like in that 'movie' about the lost boy." I tap into her essence, pulling up the name of one of her favorites. "Peter Pan. He gives the female a 'kiss'. I've heard the duke and his human mate talk about giving each other 'kisses' before and I thought—"

Hope giggles. It's such a delightful sound. "Are you talking about acorns?"

Acorn... ah. Yes. The little brown nuts. "I am. I've brought you many 'kisses'."

Her giggle becomes more of a full-throated laugh. "And here I thought I had real industrious squirrels working against me."

I furrow my brow. "I do not understand."

With her free hand, Hope waves it. "Unless you're in my brain, you wouldn't."

But I am. I have her essence... and, since I do, I know very well that this is probably the worst time to remind her of that. So I don't, choosing instead to nod sagely at her.

She smiles. It's even more beautiful than her laugh. "Anyway, those are acorns—"

"Sammael," I remind her. I had hoped for her to give me her own name for me, but for now, I just want to hear her call me anything... with the fervent belief that, one day, she'll call me hers.

"Right. Those are acorns, Sammael. They fall from the oak trees. They're not really a kiss."

"They are not?"

She shakes her head. "Nope. A kiss... well, it's when two people who are attracted to each other press their lips together because"—she shrugs—"it feels good, I guess."

Since I received Hope's essence, I allowed it to become a part of me. Because I was so sure I knew what a 'kiss' was, I never searched her thoughts and memories to verify that I was right. Now I do, and I'm bombarded by the understanding of what exactly a human kiss can be.

And, as that knowledge is absorbed next, I'm

stunned to discover that while tongues are involved, not all kisses are on the mouth...

As I'm learning about kisses, my beloved Hope stuns me by moving close enough that her naked hip brushes against my shadow coverings. Then, gazing up at me, she says, "If you want, I could show you."

If I want?

"I would be honored," I tell her solemnly.

"Okay. Here. You're a big guy so, uh, if you could lower your head so I can reach you."

I hunch so that my face is in front of hers, breathing the same air. "Like this?"

"You're so warm," she whispers softly, looking straight into my eyes. Her lips quirk into another small grin. "But, yeah. Like this. Now... I'm going to do this, okay?"

Lifting her hand, she threads her fingers through my hair, the tips of her much cooler fingers probing past my pointed ears—so different from her smooth, rounded ones—until she's resting them lightly on the side of my head.

"You got fangs," she says, pointing out the obvious. "I don't want to be cut so I'm just going to hold you in place like this. Is that alright?"

"You can do whatever you'd like," I promise her.

"God, you're so fucking cute. And I must be crazy because I'm dreaming about a monster and thinking he's cute. Okay... kiss. Open your mouth a little."

I do.

Her other hand lands on my chin. I go immovably still as she starts by pushing her soft lips against mine. She nibbles my bottom lip with her dull human teeth a few times before she slants her head, finding a new angle before she...

Oh.

She slips her tongue out of her mouth and into *mine*. The unexpected chill has me ready to shudder, but I restrain myself at the last moment. My Hope wanted me to stay still, in fear of my fangs, and I will do this for her as she leisurely strokes her tongue against mine.

But, alas, the kiss is over all too soon—and as she pulls away, panting softly, her taste left in my mouth... already I know that I will forever be addicted to this.

Letting go of my head, she grins up at me. "So? How was that?"

I marvel at my mate. "You taste delicious."

And that's just her mouth...

She taps me on my chest. "Aren't you a charmer? And an expert with your fangs, too. Look." Sticking out her tongue, she shows me the pretty pink organ before disappearing it with an impish grin on her elfin features. "Not a single nick. You sure that was your first kiss?"

Hope is teasing me, but I nod my head earnestly. "It

was," I confess. "If I could... I would like to kiss you again."

Hope shifts closer to me, tilting her head back so that I could put my mouth on hers again. "Sure."

I swallow the nervous lump in my throat. "If it pleases you, my mate, I would like to kiss you somewhere other than your mouth."

"Oh?" The small hairs over her eyes seem to lift. "Where?"

I point with my claw. "On your cunt."

HOPE

There's something about the big monster rumbling 'cunt' in his deep voice that has me about to spontaneously combust.

Now, if this wasn't one of my most fervent fantasies brought to life, there is no way I would even think about agreeing. To have a guy—whatever he is—so hooked on me that he would boldly proposition me like that? To look at me with such hunger in his eyes, like he's starving and licking my pussy is the only sustenance that will satisfy him?

His mouth is so warm. So is his skin. I thought I was dying before with how hot everything seemed, and I blamed it on the fever I woke up with this morning. Now I've been told it's *not* a fever. It's the mating sickness—but since none of this can actually be real, maybe that's my feverish brain coming up with some crazy excuse why this weirdo illness had me desperate enough to even think about sleeping with Jake.

I'm glad I didn't. While I can't deny that my co-worker would have happily followed me upstairs if I asked him to, it would've been for all the wrong reasons.

But giving in to my horniness by allowing a figment of my imagination to eat me out?

"Sure," I tell him. "Why not?"

His purple eyes glow so brightly, I nearly have to squint in the darkness of my bedroom; the only other light belongs to the full moon shining in through the gap in my black-out curtains. This close, though, I can see the hope and the hunger written in every line of his alien face.

"I can do this?"

"If you want."

"Oh, my Hope." His lips curve, showing off the inch-long fangs that gleam dangerously white against his dark mouth. "I want very much."

Sammael moves quickly. As though afraid I'll change my mind, he climbs up off of my bed, towering over me.

I'm not afraid. In fact, without my anxiety to weigh me down in my dreams, I jut my chin out, all but daring him to drop to his knees in front of me.

He doesn't. Instead, he bends slightly. His grip is

gentle yet sure as he grabs me by my hips. Just like how he was careful not to cut me with his fangs during our kiss, he purposely hoists me up with his claws reaching past me so that there's no chance that he'll accidentally poke me with those monsters.

As he moves me, laying me out so that my head is propped up against my headboard, my back cushioned by the six pillows I sleep with every night, I think that I should really be more worried about those fangs. One wrong move when he goes down on me and he could stab me in a very delicate place.

Hmm. You know… if I could sense the heat of his mouth during our kiss, and his touch earlier did something to calm whatever the hell is wrong with me, my recent dreams are even more vivid than they usually are. That means, if he does accidentally stab me, it'll hurt. Maybe… maybe this isn't the best idea.

My mattress dips as the big monster joins me on my bed. Still increasingly gentle, he lays his palms on my thighs, easing my legs open so that he can wedge his massive shoulders just beneath my spread thighs.

I shudder when his warm breath hits my exposed pussy. "Oh *God*," I moan.

He picks his head up. "I am Sammael."

He can be whoever he wants to be in my dream so long as he uses that amazingly warm tongue on me.

I don't think my fever is quite gone. Then again, maybe it is. His touch earlier definitely did something to stop the strange cramping I was suffering from all day, but compared to his heat, I'm so cold. I need his heat.

Shit, I need *him*.

And when he drops his head again, nuzzling his nose past my folds before swiping my entirely slit with the flat of his tongue, I'm burning up for a whole other reason.

I groan as he sucks in a breath, lifting his head so that I can see how much brighter his strange purple eyes are.

"Oh. Your mouth was delicious," he says in a low tone, "but your cunt... it is *delectable*."

"I, uh, I'm glad you like it."

"Like it? I *love* it."

To prove he means it, Sammael lowers his head again, nuzzling his entire face against my curls, my clit, my pussy lips before burrowing past them even more determinedly, sucking my labia into his mouth.

A keening sound escapes me as pleasure rushes through me. Sammael pins my hip with one of his huge hands, trying to keep me in place as he dips the point of his tongue just past my entrance.

Freaking hell, that feels even *better*.

I start squirming. I can't help it. Not even his one hand can keep me still, though that's probably more because my dream monster doesn't want to use his impressive strength against me.

Instead, Sammael follows my wiggling hips, almost desperate to keep his mouth on me. Since that's what I want, too, I try my best to get control but, yeah... that's a lost cause. All I want in that moment is to come. Between his enthusiasm and the oversensitivity from my earlier sickness, I'm getting close already.

I'm panting. At some point, I start saying, "I need... I *need*..." without actually verbalizing what I want from him.

I don't have to. As though he knows exactly how to work my body despite my fantasy conjuring a monster who didn't even know what a kiss was—I guess that's what happens when I hyperfixate on two different versions of Peter Pan for weeks—Sammael knows instinctively what to do. Using the side of his thumb, he puts a little pressure on my clit.

I arch my back at the sensations rushing through me. That last touch pushes me over the edge. My legs start to twitch, my climax starting at the juncture between my legs before traveling all the way down to my toes.

My whole body clenches, then relaxes as I ride out my orgasm on my monster's face.

THIS IS MY DREAM. AS SOON AS I GOT OFF LIKE THAT, I figured that it would be over. That the strangely familiar monster would disappear because he played his part. After he did, I could either knock out again, or have that same recurring dream I get all the time about it being closing time at the library but there's always one more patron coming in, shouting, "I know exactly what book I need."

Spoiler alert: they never do.

That's not what happens, though. Once I finally have to use the heel of my bare foot to nudge Sammael in the shoulder so that he would stop lapping at my pussy, I burrow cozily against my mattress as he gets up, running his hand over his mouth before he starts pacing at the end of my bed.

His eyes don't leave me. Feeling more than a little flattered by that, I don't bother covering up with the blankets.

What a guy. He's innocent enough to think an acorn is a kiss while bold enough to just come out and offer to go down on me once he gets the gist that, when it comes to kissing, tongues are involved. He calls me his mate, inferring that I'm his wife, and acts like that's some great gift to him if I really am.

Too bad he's only available in my dreams...

I sigh, watching him stalk from one side of my room to the other. "God, I wish you were real."

He pauses. "But I am real."

"In my dreams, maybe."

Shaking his head, his long, thick black hair whispering over his bare shoulder, he says, "It's true, my mate. I exist."

I wish he did.

"I exist," he repeats, "but only to you. You cannot see me when you're not dreaming. You cannot touch me. But I am there."

He sounds so earnest that I would feel bad—even in my dreams—shutting him down without giving him a chance to talk me into believing that he *could* be real.

If everything he says is true... "You mean, like a ghost?"

"I was a demon. A Sombran demon. Now... now I am a phantom." Sammael is quiet for a moment before he nods this time. "A phantom is like a ghost, so yes. When we're not on the dream-plane, I am a ghost."

Wouldn't that just explain everything? Oh, no, Hope. You're not crazy. You're just being haunted by a fantasy lover who is a huge fan of pussy and has a pair of demon horns.

Of course. That's what he just said. He's a demon—

Wait a minute. I'm not saying I believe this... but he didn't just say he was a demon. He said he was a *Sombra* demon. And where have I seen that word lately?

Oh, how about that weird leather-bound book with the pentacle on the front, and the title page calling itself the *Grimoire du Sombra*? The very same book that has been freaking *following* me around?

And he's trying to tell me he's a ghost?

"Have you been watching me or something?"

"I've been protecting you. Helping you."

"How?"

"I brought you the spellbook," Sammael says. "You kept bringing it back to the library. I can only touch things that my mate touched, or items from Sombra, so I made sure to retrieve it for you whenever you did."

What?

"That was you? I thought I was going nuts!"

"I'm sorry, my mate." He takes a few steps toward me. "If I upset you, I'm so sorry... but I needed you to have it. The book. I should've told you already—"

It is what it is. If he's really been following me... if he really is a ghost... I have more important things to worry about. "Have you seen me naked?"

I don't think he was expecting such a quick change of subject, but he answers me right away all the same. "Yes."

I scramble away from him, grasping for my blanket. Sure, I didn't mind him watching me *now*, but if he's been peeking at me for a while before, that's not cool. That's not cool at all.

The monster—demon—ghost... *whatever* frowns. "I pointed out that you were uncovered, my mate. You were the one who said they were just tits."

First 'cunt', now 'tits' instead of the way he called them 'breasts' before... if he doesn't stop talking like that, I might forget that I'm upset and let him look all he wants some more.

Wait a second—

"Do you mean, like, now?" I wave my hand up and down at my body. "Is this the first time you saw me like this?"

His expression turns so hurt, he makes me think of a puppy who's just gotten kicked. "I would never take what you did not freely offer. No matter how long I had to wait, I would earn my first glimpse of your beauty."

Wow. Now I feel bad for assuming he was some kind of demon perv. Even so, that still doesn't mean he should get a pass for *haunting* me for... for...

Well, I don't know how long, but I should probably find out.

"Let me ask you something. You've been watching me—"

"Protecting you," he repeats.

Sure. "For how long? How long have you been doing this?"

I'd like to say that last night's dream was the first time I ever saw a creature like him in my imagination... but it wasn't. Just like I've been dealing with this strange feeling that someone was behind me, calling my name, calling me to them even before that weird book showed up at the library, I've seen a monster similar to Sammael in my daydreams for ages.

Not to mention how I've thought I've been going crazy for months now...

"Four cycles," Sammael admits.

Cycles?

"Months," he amends. "Humans refer to them as months."

"Four *months*? And you only just decided to tell me this?"

"Oh, Hope... you only just started to call me to you."

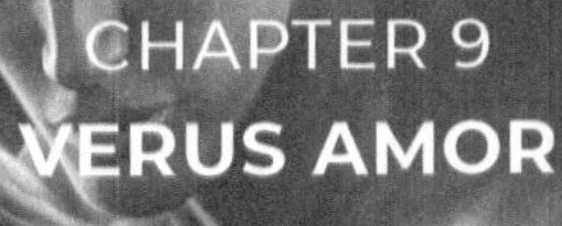

CHAPTER 9
VERUS AMOR

HOPE

I was so worried that I would wake up the next morning and still feel like garbage.

To my surprise, I don't. I actually feel more relaxed than I have in ages, and if I didn't have a vivid recollection of the disappointment flashing across Jake's face as I all but booted him out my front door, I'd second-guess if I got lucky last night.

I know I didn't bother pulling out my vibe, either. As shitty as I felt all day and night, I remember passing out, hoping that fourteen hours of sleep was just what I needed to shake it off.

Looks like I was right. Stretching my arms, snuggling back into my pillow, I decide it had to be some weird twenty-four-hour bug.

I mean, what's the alternative? That my vivid sex dream from last night, when I conjured the monster of my fantasies and ended up riding his face to an explosive orgasm, was actually real? That the mate sickness I imagined was making me so hot and horny that, if he whipped out his dick, I might have decided to ride that next?

Despite how real it seemed like it was at the time, it was just a dream. Unconscious Hope was attracted to the horned demon with the purple eyes for two reasons: one) because it's closing in on Halloween and this is the season to let my monsterfucker freak flag fly, and two) because I came up with him, putting him in the starring role of my fantasies, so why wouldn't I want to fuck him?

I've never really had a type. Now, I won't say I'm not shallow and that looks don't play a part. They do. There has to be something about a guy that turns me on otherwise why would I waste my time, right? But I can be drawn to a lanky, somewhat nerdy yet undeniably good-looking librarian one moment, then be ready to be naked with a seven-foot-tall demon with horns and muscles so hard, I could take a bite out of them the next. Jake and my imaginary demon are as different as night and day when it comes to appearance, but personality...

I'm a big personality gal. To me, that trumps everything else. I like thoughtful. I like sweet. I like earnest...

basically, give me your golden retriever-types and your cinnamon rolls, and I'm basically done for.

Jake's persistence never really bothered me because I knew that, at the end of the day, he always respected my 'no'. When I was firm about it, he backed off, but then he'd send me a video because he said it made him think of me, or off-handedly quote Whiskey Rose lyrics at me... and, whoops. I started to wonder 'what-if' again.

My monster, though... I remember how, in my dream, I told him that I wished he was 'real'. As I reach over, grabbing my phone and checking the time, sighing in relief when I see that I still have ten minutes before I have to be in the shower to get ready for work, I have to admit that I still kinda do.

What kind of woman doesn't want an otherworldly demon who looks at her as though she hung the freaking moon before just about begging to eat her out? And the way he was still so sweet, getting the idea that a 'kiss' was an acorn from one of my favorite movies?

That's another reason why I know that I created him out of my subconsciousness. A gentle giant who is charmed enough by Peter Pan to think it's real? Who then tries to show his affection for me by leaving acorns on my porch because he's a 'ghost' who can't reach me any other way but my dreams?

Yeah, right.

I just took the squirrels' tendency to leave acorns in my way and turned it into something sweet, that's all.

Still, can't deny that that was a pretty spicy dream I had. Whether it was an aftereffect from my strange bug that had me horny as hell, I'm not sure, but at least I'm not sick anymore.

I'll take what I can get.

I'M STILL IN A GREAT MOOD AFTER I DRAG MY BUTT OUT of bed and take a quick shower so that I can get ready for work. That done, I'm thinking about whether I should splurge and get a bagel and a cup of tea at Dunkin' or if I should brew some of my own at home.

Green tea does wonders for me. I switch to coffee when I need the caffeine boost, but I prefer green tea—and sometimes black tea—as a pick-me-up to start my day.

Checking my phone, I see that there's enough time to eat at my house. I probably should. Eating out with Jake last night wasn't part of my budget, and I'd be better off saving the couple of bucks I'd spend on breakfast for another day.

However, as I jog down my stairs, about to head through my living room so that I can get to my kitchen, I stop short when I notice that something is resting on the top of my couch.

It's that book. It's that *damn* book that, I swear to God, was following me from the library and back for a few days until I finally gave up and shoved it under my bed. Figuring it was out of sight, out of mind, I purposely tried to forget about it... and actually managed to for a bit.

My heart jumps when I see it. One thing for sure, I know I didn't drop to my knees, crawl under my bed, grab the book, and bring it downstairs. I definitely didn't crack it open to one particular page toward the back of the book, either.

But someone did.

My first instinct is to grab the book, slam it closed, and maybe toss it in the trash this time. I'd like to see it find its way back to my house after being buried under tons of garbage in the local landfill. Only... the second I reach for it, I can't help but glance down at the page.

Then, because it was inevitable, I read the top of it.

I already knew that the entire book was written in a foreign language. I finally tried to run a couple of portions of the early pages through my translation app, but it came back as legit gobbledy-gook. I didn't bother again after that.

This page, though? It looks like someone might have cracked part of the code.

At the top, there are two words in bold: **VERUS AMOR.** But that's not all.

True love...

That's what's written beneath the printed letters. As though someone had translated the foreign language above it, they make it clear what this page is supposed to be: a 'true love' spell.

And the demon from my dreams told me that I'm his wife.

No—his *mate*.

Does that mean I'm supposed to be his true love, too?

Because the gods gave you to me. You were fated to be mine...

Holy shit. Holy *shit*.

I wish you were real...

I am...

The book belongs to the monster in my dreams. Sammael. He admitted to that, just like he admitted that he's the one who's basically been haunting me. I mean, he told me he was a ghost. He told me he has spent four months watching me, waiting for me to call him. To... to *summon* him.

My trembling fingers trail down the page before tapping the word 'manifest' scrawled in the margin. The first passage is starred, with 'manifest' hand-written next to it; the second part is marked by the word 'promise'. I have no idea what that means, but it's obviously some kind of message.

I choke, one part sob, one part hysterical laughter bursting free from me. If this is a message, it's gotta be from the demon who went down on me—and what the hell am I supposed to do about that?

I don't know. I... I just don't freaking know.

But I'm a younger sister. My whole life, whenever there was something I didn't know, I had one reaction: get Johanna.

My phone is in the back pocket of my jeans. Leaving the book where it is, I yank it out and hurriedly select my sister's contact name on my list of recent calls.

Please pick up, please pick up...

"Hello?"

I exhale, gripping my phone tightly. "Jo. It's me."

As if the picture of me didn't pop up on the screen when her phone rang. I'm too frazzled to think clearly, though, and—for once—my older sister doesn't tease me about it. She doesn't remind me that she's probably in the middle of teaching, either.

She must hear something in my voice because hers drops. "What's wrong, Hope?"

How do I explain?

In true *me* fashion, I blurt it out: "I thought I was going crazy, but now I think I have. Because, Jo... I'm being *haunted*."

Thank God for Johanna Megill.

My sister doesn't even hesitate. She doesn't ask questions. If she thinks I'm having some kind of mental health crisis—or if I'm pulling a Halloween prank a week early—she keeps those thoughts to herself. Sure, maybe she's doing that because I got her in the middle of her first period and she had to get me off the phone, but she promises to meet up with me tonight after we both get out of work.

I double-check my schedule. I swear, if it said that I was working with Jake today, I would've called out. I would've been able to handle him if it was just a weird dream last night, but if this is real... if *Sammael* is real... there's no way I have the mental power to deal with Jake's puppy dog eyes when I'm pretty sure I'm still losing my damn mind.

I knew I was working from ten to six which is why my sister said to expect her around six-thirty. Looking at my screen, I see that Moira's off. So is Jake today. Victoria is the lead library tech, with two of the new girls working the morning and afternoon shifts.

That's fine. Besides, if I used yesterday's illness as an excuse to call out today, I'd just sit in my house, staring into each corner, wondering if there's an attractive monster watching my every move.

He is, isn't he? If I admit that he really found a way to visit me in my dreams, then he's gotta be here somewhere, waiting to see if I picked up on his most recent hint.

There's been plenty, I have to admit. All those times I swore there was someone lurking just out of sight. The way the book constantly followed me. Little things, like my slippers being moved or how my remote fell off the couch, followed by my front door flying open yesterday... what if the demon ghost was responsible for all of it?

That's all I'm thinking about as I'm sleepwalking through my shift. About halfway through, it suddenly hits me that the monster mentioned that he visited the library to steal the book back for me. Is he here now, I wonder. Did he follow me to work?

If he did, he doesn't give any sign that he's here. Even when I give in and whisper, "Sammael," out loud, the only thing that happens is that a nearby patron glances up from their book and shushes me.

It's a relief when my shift's finally over and I get to go home. I drove today because the idea of walking home at night in late October with a freaking *ghost* at my back had me even more spooked. Besides, I want to be inside, waiting for Johanna, when she gets to my house.

At six-thirty on the dot, Johanna swans through the door, carrying a pizza box with another, longer box stacked on top of it. It's not her style to knock, and knowing she was coming, I purposely left the door unlocked, though she has a key to my place.

I'm sitting on my couch, bare feet nervously

tapping the hardwood floor as I stare at the spellbook. When I came home earlier, I found that it had moved again. The book was closed, waiting for me on the coffee table I got for twenty bucks from Facebook Marketplace. It has divots in the wood and it lists to one side, but I usually keep it around so I have somewhere to put my drink when I'm watching a movie.

Tonight, it's holding the spellbook—and, later, the two boxes Johanna brought with her.

"Mark's watching the twins," she announces as she flips open the first box, grabbing a slice of pizza. "I told my husband we had girl stuff to take care of and he decided to take them to Fright Fest before it gets too crowded. I can stay as long as you need me, okay? But, before we get into the ghost stuff, eat. You look pale as hell, Hope."

I'm usually pale, but I appreciate the concern. Taking a slice of my own, I work to get it down without my nervous belly getting in the way. After taking a bite, I jerk my chin at the second box. "Please tell me you didn't bring a Ouija board with you."

"Why not? You said you were haunted, right? I figure... if you are, maybe we can call the other side and tell them to leave you the fuck alone."

"You don't believe in any of that paranormal stuff."

"No, but you do. And if this is what I have to do to support my baby sister, I'll do it."

See? That's exactly why I called Johanna in the first

place. I don't know anyone else who would ship her kids off with her husband just so she can bring me pizza and play into my delusions like this. Sure, if it turns out I *am* nuts, she'll do anything to get me the help I need… but, first, she's going to do this.

We might as well get started.

Well, once we finish polishing off half the pizza…

As she sets up the Ouija board and the planchette on the coffee table, she nods at the *Grimoire du Sombra*. "Is that the book you think is following you?"

It *is* following me. "Yes."

"Good. Let's leave it there. Maybe it'll help when we call on your ghost."

It's worth a shot. Dropping to my knees on the other side of the coffee table, I wait until Jo gives me a signal, then follow her lead, laying my fingers on the plastic planchette.

My fingers zap the instant they touch it.

Cursing under my breath, I take them back—but before Jo can ask me what's wrong, the spellbook opens, the pages flipping quickly before they land specifically on the same exact page it was on this morning.

"Whoa." Johanna scrambles up to her feet, pointing down at the book. "Did that just fucking happen?"

Yes. Yes it did. Because I'm haunted, and my brilliant older sister decided to bring a freaking Ouija board into my house.

Without even waiting for my answer, she crouches low, running her gaze over the page. "What... what is this?"

I know I must sound nuts, but I tell her, "I think it's a true love spell."

"What?" Excitement fills my sister's voice. "Oh my God. We have to try it!"

"Johanna—"

"No, seriously. I mean, I don't think it'll work... but I didn't really think the Ouija board would do anything, either. You have to do it."

Me? I push the book toward Jo. "No. You do it!"

She shoves it back. "I can't. I'm already married."

I raise my eyebrows. "Mark Megill is really your true love?"

"And the father of my kids, thank you," Johanna answers readily. "But you're single and ready to mingle. A dead guy can't be any worse than some of the losers you've dated."

He's not dead. He's just... a phantom demon from another realm who can follow me into my dreams.

"Fine." I give in. If Johanna really thinks I should do this... "Look. There are some instructions written at the bottom. It says... it says we need to use some salt to form a protective circle."

"Makes sense. Okay. Go grab some from the

kitchen."

I can't believe I'm really doing this. Even as I go up on my tip-toes, grabbing the big container of salt I use to refill my shakers, I can't believe I'm doing this... but that doesn't stop me.

Setting the salt down on the coffee table, I look at the bottom of the page again. "Hmmm... I know I don't have any chalk. What about you?"

With a strangely sarcastic look, Johanna pats her pockets. "Nope. Sorry. Fresh out."

"Really? You're a teacher. Why don't you have chalk?"

"Maybe because we rarely use the stuff these days? It's all computers at the school. Besides, you're a librarian. Does that mean you always carry a book with you? And this haunted one doesn't count."

Oh, Johanna. You really should've known the answer to that one.

Without looking away from my sister, I go and grab my purse. After digging around inside of it for a moment, I pull out my e-reader and my emergency paperback I carry just in case I forget to charge my Kindle and it dies. Raising my eyebrows, I show them both to Johanna.

She sticks her tongue out at me.

Snorting under my breath, I stow my book and my Kindle back in my bag. "Real mature, Jo."

"Hey. I'm not the one who insists they're being

haunted."

I already got the chance earlier to explain myself as soon as I got out of work. Johanna called me on her drive up from her house in Helmetta. A forty-five-minute ride up to Westfield, she kept me talking for at least twenty of those minutes, alternating between teasing me now that I'm not obviously freaking out, asking detailed questions—though I refuse to tell her about what I let the monster do to me... or the fact that it's a horned *demon* who might be haunting me—about why I think I am being haunted, and talking me down when I start to ramp up again.

That's another thing to love about my sister. If you asked her yesterday if she believed in ghosts, she'd wave her hand and shake her head. Today? Because I seem so sure of it, she shows up with pizza for dinner and an Ouija board.

I point at the open book. "If I'm not haunted, how do you explain that?"

"I don't," she agrees easily. "Sorry, Hope, but I'm pretty sure you *are* being haunted. At the very least, someone or something wants you to read that spell over there. So... are you gonna?"

You know what? I am. Hopefully, when nothing happens, I can chalk this up to one really, really weird evening. Maybe then I can fall asleep and imagine talking to Sammael again, and he can try to explain why my subconscious is so obsessed with that book.

If he's not real, his answer will come straight from me. And if he *is* real...

I grab the salt from Johanna and start shaking it on the floor. I don't have any chalk to draw the protective sigil on the page—and here's hoping nothing bad will happen if I don't—so I swirl the container of salt around my head a couple of times like I've suddenly turned into Allison from the old Disney classic, *Hocus Pocus*.

That done, I set the container of salt on the coffee table, then heft up the book.

"Here goes nothing," I murmur, turning my attention to the first part of the spell.

And 'nothing' is exactly what happens as I stumble through the first few unfamiliar lines, but I've come too far to stop now. And then, when I'm just about done with the *manifest* section, the strangest freaking thing happens.

My door is shut. So are my windows. There is no reason why my living room should have a gale-force wind whipping around it, or a mass of dark shadows welling in one corner before it begins to grow and grow.

Pausing, I glance over at my sister. "Should I stop?"

"No, keep going," Johanna says, raising her voice over the wind. Excitement lights up her features. "I want to see what happens."

I don't think I do—but I start to read the next part... the *promise*... anyway.

Just as I'm reciting the last line of the second paragraph, the shadows condense in on themselves. Impossibly black except for a pair of glowing purple lights standing out from the darkness about a foot above my head, they're there for a moment before they shift to a different creature entirely.

Behind me, Johanna starts screaming.

Honestly? If I had never seen him before, I probably would, too.

The creature that steps out of the shadows is huge. Like, *massive*. A good seven feet tall if I'm any judge, with the horns sticking out of the top of his head adding at least eight inches to his height. His muscles are huge, his chest is huge, and if he wasn't wearing the wafting, thick black shadows starting at his waist like a tailored pair of pants, I'm betting the dick he's packing is really freaking huge.

And considering where our last interlude left off last night, there's a pretty good chance that he wants to use it on me... because I have seen him before.

I freaking kissed him, then let him go down on me.

He said he was a phantom.

He thinks I'm his *wife*.

And I just summoned him into my living room after reading something that was called a 'true love' spell.

SAMMAEL

At last, I am whole again.

After meeting her on the dream-plane the night before, my Hope finally understood that—when we are on Earth together—I *am* a phantom. Now that I made her aware that the *Grimoire du Sombra* was meant for her, I used as much of my energy as I could spare to retrieve it from under her bedding, then left it open to the *verus amor* spell.

I had done so before. Each time, Hope immediately shut the cover, unaware that the only way to manifest me—to return both my forms *and* my magic—would be with that incantation.

But, almost as though she was rewarding me for giving her such pleasure during the time of shadows, once she left the dream-plane this morning, she actually looked at the spell.

Then, hours later when she returned to her quarters with her kin coming to visit, the two females decided that my Hope should read it. Not only did she manifest me, but by forging on and reciting the mate's promise in her own voice, all we must do is complete the essence exchange and finalize our bond by physically mating—my cock in her cunt, my seed filling her up—and we will be forever mates.

I had every intention of explaining that to my Hope as soon as I finished manifesting in the human realm.

I made one big miscalculation, though. In my haste to shift from my shadow form to my demon shape, I momentarily forgot that it wasn't solely Hope who was waiting for me in her world.

Her kin—who looks enough like my Hope that it's obvious they're relations, though my Hope is infinitely more lovely—begins to scream the moment I step out of the shadows and beneath the artificial light of Hope's quarters.

My mate does not. She watches me with a mixture of confusion and surprise as I throw up my demon hands, freezing her kin in place.

Ah. It's so good to have my magic back... or so I believe until, in the next moment, Hope *does* begin to shout.

It's not the unintelligible yell of fright like her kin.

Instead, she rushes forward, calling the other female's name—"Johanna! Jo!"—before she whirls on me. "What did you do to my sister?"

"Be at ease," I tell her, trying to soothe her. Through our fledgling bond, I can sense her upset. That is not what I intended, but I had no other choice. "The duke's first law is that no other human can know that Sombra exists. Only a mate can. You are my mate, beloved. Your kin... your *sister*... is not."

She shakes her head. "I don't know what the hell any of that means, but whatever the fuck you did, you better fix her!"

I can do that. Momentarily closing my eyes, I use magic to erase everything Hope's kin has learned from her about Sombra, followed by the sight of myself emerging from the shadows in my demon form. I pluck out the memory of the *Grimoire du Sombra* and the *verus amor* spell, then plant the suggestion that her visit to my mate's home will be nothing but a dream after she returns to her own.

That done, I open my eyes and gesture at the female, though not before I fade completely to the faintest of my shadows so there's no way she can see me.

Like Hope, she has eyes the same shade as Duke Haures. She blinks them a few times, then smiles at my mate. "Wow. Look at the time. I got almost an hour's drive back to Helmetta, and that's hoping there's not traffic on the Parkway. It was good seeing you, Hope. If you're not busy, you should really see if you can stop by for the twins' Halloween parade next week."

Hope glances over to where I was last. Her brow is furrowed, her lips pulled downward, but when she looks at Johanna again, she forces a grin. "Yeah, Jo. That sounds great. Tell 'em I can't wait to see them."

"They're going as Barbie and Ken. It's adorable."

"I'm sure it is." One last glance thrown my way, then Hope accompanies her kin to the front door. "Text me when you get home, okay? Be safe."

"You, too. And don't spend too much of your time worrying about those break-ins anymore. I know you get worked up over things like that, but if it helps, I can get you one of those doorbell cameras for Christmas. Think about it, okay?"

Hope frowns again, probably because we both know that that was not why she called her sister over for help earlier, but she says nothing. Instead, she waves the other female off. Only after Johanna is gone does she shut the door behind her, then face me again.

I shift back to my demon skin. It's what she knows me best as after these last two nights together, and I want to make sure she recognizes me outside of the dream-plane.

Her hands go straight to her hips. "Sammael."

Ah. So she *does* remember me. "Yes, my mate?"

She winces when I call her that. She shouldn't.

After giving me the mating promise, vowing to give herself to me forever, she is even *more* my mate than she was before... but I keep that to myself as she peers up at me. "You fixed her... kinda... but I still want to know what you did to Jo."

"All I did was erase any knowledge of Sombra from her for her own safety. She is not a mate. Her true love is a Mark," I remind Hope. I was listening, waiting to see if she would cast the manifestation spell, and ready to swoop the book away if Hope's kin attempted the magic herself. "Your true love is Sammael. We are not in breach of the duke's first law."

"You can do that? And then, what? You gave her a nudge to go home so that we could have this little chat? Because I am..." She shakes her head, as though unable to call herself what she is: my mate. "You can do that?"

That's only the beginning of the magic I can wield now that I am whole again. "Of course. I am a mage."

"Like a wizard? I thought you were a demon." Hope frowns. "I thought you were a *ghost.*"

"I was a phantom," I correct gently.

"Same thing."

To a human, perhaps. To a Sombra demon, being forced to exist as a phantom, able to watch but unable to touch... it was the price I had to pay for both my hubris and my impatience.

I only wish that it's the only one I'll have to pay...

I refuse to think about that for now. Not with the memory of Hope's taste on my tongue, and the way my whole essence sings to know that she has given herself to me. It insists that I do the same. Already, I've made my mating vow to her countless times, even when she couldn't hear me, but I held back from giving her my essence until she was ready to accept it.

She is now. At least, I *believe* she is—and even if she isn't, I can answer all of her questions... make her understand everything about how I feel and what it means to be a Sombra demon's mate... if only she'll take my essence in return.

I hold out my hand. "Touch me."

"No, no, no." She holds hers up, warding me off. "I did that before. In my dream, remember? And that's when all this crazy shit really started."

She is wrong about that. This all started the moment I took the spellbook from Loki, betraying Duke Haures by stealing it for my own instead of leaving it in the human realm for another mortal to find.

But Hope still doesn't know that... yet.

I wiggle my fingers. "Please, Hope."

"'Please'," she echoes, huffing under her breath. "That's how you got me last time, too."

"If you take my hand, I can share myself with you. That's all I ask." For now. "Accept my essence and, I promise you, you'll have the answer to any question you wish to ask me right in your grasp."

She hesitates. "*Any* answer?"

There are no secrets between mates. She will know everything about me once she has my essence, the good and the bad, and all she'll have to do is search herself to know the truth.

I would give it to her regardless. Though I'm not proud of everything I have done in my life, I *am* proud of my love and affection for her. I want her to know how much I care, and that there's no rush. I desire to make her my forever mate, and as long as I do before the gold moon, I will get to keep her.

We have time. Time for her to learn me and decide to make me hers. For me? I made my choice four cycles ago... and there is nothing—or *almost* nothing—that will keep me from my Hope.

And, as she inches toward me, holding out her hand at last, she shall finally understand that.

One touch. That's all it takes. When Hope gave me her essence, it was only because she didn't know that the exchange would happen the first time she brushed her soft skin against mine. All Sombra demons know how to guard their essence until it's time to give it away to their mates.

Like I do now.

Yanking her hand back quickly, I know that my

essence took root inside of my female the moment her eyes go wide as she stares up at me.

I smile down at her encouragingly.

Hope does not smile back. "You... you're a demon. An immortal demon." She swallows roughly. "Holy shit. You're, like, a thousand years old!"

Not quite. "I have seen nine centuries so far."

That doesn't seem to help.

"I'm twenty-eight!"

"Yes. You are a mature female. I am a mature male."

"And you want to fuck me!"

Fuck... using her essence, I try to understand what she means and nod knowingly when I realize that she's talking about the physical act of mating.

"I must. Whenever you are willing to accept me, I will do my best to pleasure you as I fill your cunt with my cock. Then you will be my bonded mate. Not a mortal any longer, but *mine*. And I promise you, my Hope, for the rest of our existence together, I will always love you. I will keep you safe. You will want for nothing... and all I want is you."

Her mouth drops open. For a moment, it looks like she's about to say something, but she doesn't. Instead, stumbling around her furniture, she allows herself to fall onto the cushioning.

This is to be expected. I've heard of those who needed a moment to process the essence exchange.

With as many centuries I have seen, there's a lot for Hope to learn about me and my existence.

As a good mate, I walk over to her and, in an attempt to show her that I care, I pat her gently on the top of her head.

She squeaks, peeking up at me.

"Stay here, my mate. Let me take care of you."

I wait for her to respond. When all she does is gulp again, then nod, I pat her once more before heading purposely toward the room where she prepares all of her meals.

MY MATE IS VULNERABLE. SHE CAN BE HURT.

That's the undeniable truth. Until we bond, my beloved Hope is still mortal. She can die. Even if she doesn't, if any harm comes to her, she cannot heal herself in the shadows like I can. She is too, too vulnerable—and that worries me.

As her male, though, it is my responsibility to tend to her. And though she is well for the moment, I can sense her confusion through our bond. She doesn't know what to make of me—or our future mating—and has retreated inside of herself, looking for answers.

I can provide her all of them with my essence, but to prove that I'm a male who deserves her, there is more that I can do right now.

I will show her that I can take care of her better than any of her mortal lovers have. I am her one true mate. I know her heart—and that means I also know what will soothe her in this moment.

And, though it takes me longer than it does her, I move easily back into her living quarters, offering her the wee cup held gingerly between my claws.

"For you, my mate."

Hope glances up. She has eased back into her seat, more content than before, and I see the curious look in her pretty eyes as she notices what I'm holding.

"What's that?"

Doesn't she know?

"Hot leaf water," I tell her proudly.

She giggles. The sound makes my heart—and my cock—swell. "What did you say?"

Hot leaf water... that's what I made for her.

I've watched her prepare it countless times when I was still a phantom. She would take a kettle, fill it with water, and heat it over the fire she keeps inside of that big white square in her kitchen. That part wasn't necessary for me. I used a pulse of magic from my palm to make the water steam, then dropped a pinch of her green leaves into the cup. After giving it a stir with my pointer claw, I brought it to my Hope.

She's still sitting on the couch where I left her, though her mood seems much improved now than when I left her a few moments ago. With the smoking mug in her hand, I sense a rush of affection and humor coming down our bond to me.

My chest puffs up in pride. I knew I could show my mate how good of a male I can be to her!

I know why she drinks this. It is like javits, a brewed beverage from my world that provides energy and stamina to those who partake in it. It makes her happy.

I want to, as well.

"For you," I repeat, holding the mug out to her still. "Your boiled leaves. The ones you like to drink sometimes."

She finally takes the mug, easing it out of my grip. Peeking inside, she says, "Heavy on the leaves, huh?"

I just did what she did. I grabbed a pinch between my claws and dropped it into her cup. "Did I use too many?"

"No," she lies. To save my pride, she fibs. And I know that it is a fib because her tiny nose wrinkles as she sniffs her cup, then leans forward to place the mug on her even tinier table. "Thanks."

I sink down so that I'm on her level. "How are you feeling, Hope? And, please, be honest with me."

I don't mean to call her out on her fib, but as much as I appreciate my Hope trying to spare my feelings, I would prefer our mating did not start out with my mate lying no matter her reason.

She can tell. From her side of the bond, my earnestness reaches her.

She nods. "Better," she says at last. "A little shocked before, but when you gave me a couple of minutes to sit here, sifting through your memories... I think I'm beginning to understand what's going on. You..." She shifts so that we're looking at each other. Her finger lands on my shoulder. "You're real, Sammael."

Just one fleeting touch is enough to have me ready to spill my seed. I've waited nine centuries to claim my mate, and for the first time since I've found her in my Hope, I am whole, she is aware of me, and our unfulfilled mating promises are already pushing me to find my way inside of her.

I must control myself. If I could make it nine centuries before mating, I can give Hope as much time as she needs to either accept me—or deny me. As long as it's before the gold moon, that is...

She's watching me closely, as though she could look right past my eyes and see into my heart.

"So... I really am your mate, huh?"

"Yes. And, one day soon, I hope you'll be my bonded mate."

"What's the difference?" Then, before I can answer, she says, "Look. I know you told me that touching you would give me all the answers, but you didn't mention it would be like this download about you right into my brain. It's too much—especially the part where you seem convinced that we're these fated partners who are meant for each other. How... how is that even possible?"

"It's part of being demonkind," I explain. "You gave me your essence. After I gave you mine, we are tied together."

"Like soul mates?"

I think about that for a moment. Hope understands the concept of 'essence' as similar to a human 'soul'. In that case... "Yes."

She nods. "Okay. I think I got you so far. And that whole thing the other day... that mate sickness that made me feel like I needed to hump anyone? That's because I'm really supposed to be humping you?"

Hope has such an odd way of putting things. Eventually, it'll be easier for us to understand each other. As her grasp of Sombran becomes more instinctive, and I learn more of her human tongue, the translations will be more exact. For now, I think about what she's saying for a moment before—

"Are you asking me if the gods have decided that you are the only female I will ever pleasure?"

The heights of her pale cheeks turn red. It's not as vivid as a Sombra demon's coloring, but it makes her impossibly more alluring to me. "Yeah. I guess I am."

"Then, yes. It's how demons are made. We are given heightened senses. Strength. An immortal existence. However, we only have one true mate. If we choose to forsake her, taking another, and then we find her... we only have one true mate, but we also can only bond one mate to us. If I gave my essence to another, I would not have any for you. So I waited... and whether you accept me or not, you are the only female I will ever be allowed to pleasure. And now that I found you, know this: even if I could choose another, I wouldn't. You are perfect for me, and I will strive to be perfect for *you*."

Hope is watching me closely, trying to read my face, making sure I'm being honest now.

I am. With her, I always will be.

She taps her fingers against her thigh. "So... and I'm just making sure I understand this... but you can't, like, *cheat* or anything? No divorce. No separation. You're immortal... what about me?"

"When we are bonded, you shall be immortal, too. A demon's mate is forever, my beloved. If you choose me... *we* will be forever."

She's quiet for a few more seconds, and then she says, "No one else is allowed to know about you. Does that mean, as your mate, you'll expect me to go live in your demon world with you? 'Cause I got a glimpse of it in your download thing and... I'm a homebody. I like *my* home. I don't think I can live in Hell."

"Sombra."

"Same thing."

I don't argue. This 'Hell' she refers to is fairly similar to Sombra if her essence is anything to go by.

"When I left Sombra, searching for my female... for my mate... for *you*... I knew there might be a chance I wouldn't be returning any time soon. It was my home, but now? My home is with my Hope."

"So... again, just checking... but that sickness from the other day? That's because I'm your mate, but we haven't slept together yet? And that, when we do, not only will that stop happening, but I get a gorgeous demon for a forever husband, who will never cheat, never stray, never get tired of me watching the same damn movie every night... and we can stay here?"

"Yes. Yes, all that is correct," I tell her.

"Oh." She leans back into her seat, then pushes forward, rising to her feet. "Okay, then. Let's go."

CHAPTER 11
TEA

HOPE

Later, I'll admit to myself it was the tea that did it. To a certain degree, the memory of those acorns, plus how he used magic to keep Johanna from getting caught in the crosshairs of the ruler of his demon world helped, too, as well as the many, many benefits I'd get by deciding to hook up with him... but, if I'm being truthful, it was the tea.

Sammael went into my kitchen and, like my mom used to do when I was upset, he brewed me a cup of tea. And, sure, he basically threw some of the loose leaves into some hot water and handed it to me with a look of intense pride, but I don't care about that. I don't care that I couldn't drink it, or that he knew I was full of it when I told him he did it right.

The fact that he did it at all? That he learned from watching me because I matter to him?

I've been drawn to him from the first time he walked into my dreams. I told myself I made him up, and as I stand there, looking up at him now, I still wonder if maybe I did.

Almost two weeks ago, I asked myself a question: *how do I know if I'm going crazy?* I swore I was being haunted—and I was right. I swore that old book was following me around. It was. And I honestly believed that I imagined Sammael because why else would a creature like him want me?

Is it because we're fated? If that was the case, I'd put an end to this just as easily as I turned down Jake all those times before. Me being his one true mate might be the reason why he's here, why he searched for me at all, but is that why he patted me on the head and went to my kitchen to make me a cup of undrinkable tea?

Is that why he brought me acorns and—with a very recent memory of his running through my mind—was the reason why my remote fell, my picture knocked over, and my front door opened the night I invited my co-worker back to my place?

Sammael was jealous. Not because the mate sickness made me so desperate to turn to any other guy since he was obviously unavailable, but simply because another male could touch his Hope.

Not his mate.

His beloved Hope.

Me.

He wants *me*.

There's one huge bonus to him giving me his essence. Before the overload of information basically short-circuited my brain, giving me a massive headache until I stopped digging through it, I learned enough from him to know that this... it's legit.

Seems like we also have a deadline he's being careful not to tell me so that I don't feel rushed into a lifetime commitment, but it's all real.

The big demon keeps mentioning this duke of his, and something called the 'first law'. All I get from my sneaky forays into that dump of info he dropped into my brain is that the duke of Sombra is in charge of Sammael's demon realm, and that anyone who breaks that law—showing themselves off to the human world —ends up as his prisoner.

Chains might be involved, too, and that freaks me out so much, I quickly stop thinking about it—a feat I can only accomplish because, holy shit, there are so many other things commanding my attention since I learned that Sammael is real, and he really, really wants to keep me.

Three nights ago, while I was picking a Halloween movie, I watched Casper for the first time in ages.

Can I keep you?

I'd blame the movie for Sammael's innate insistence on making me his forever mate after haunting me all these months... but I can't. His essence assures me that he's considered me *his* from the moment he read the *verus amor* spell himself and forged a tie between us that led him to haunting me for months.

The funny thing is, if he learned anything from *my* essence, it's that the one thing that tempts my anxious, scattered brain more than anything is stability.

It's why I eat the same foods. Watch the same movies constantly. Have the same job, walk the same path, and get the same order at Dunkin' when I can afford it.

Forever with the same guy who adores me and will never grow tired of me because that's now how his kind is wired?

Sign me the fuck up.

Besides, it's not like I didn't already let him touch me. I can try to tell myself that I thought I was dreaming all I wanted, that I've always been a vivid dreamer, but the moment he invited me to touch him —the way he screwed up his alien features just to say the word *please*—it was all too real.

The way his eyes plead with me to mean what I'm so clearly offering him now... that's real, too.

I hold out my hand. Sammael places his in mine, instinctively trusting me.

He's twice my size. He has claws and fangs, horns

and pointed ears, and a body that could do real damage if he wanted to. But he doesn't… I mean, he wants to use his gorgeous body *on* me, *with* me, but he will never, ever purposely hurt me.

And that's all I need to know.

I tug on his arm. I could never take him anywhere he doesn't want to go, and I can sense his big body humming as I lead him out of the living room and up the stairs.

As we go, I have a question. I already know the answer. However, since it's suddenly important that I hear it for myself, to make sure we're on the same page here, I ask, "Have you ever done this before? Mated?"

"I waited for my mate, Hope. I waited for *you*."

I have a hard time getting a good grasp on exactly how old he is, but the fact that he measures his age in *centuries* instead of *years* tells me that my demon isn't just otherworldly, he's immortal; a moment later, another answer slides into my brain, assuring me that he *is* immortal… and if I bang him, I will be, too.

Forget that last part for now. Sammael is close to being a thousand years old… and he's gone all that time without having sex because he was waiting for *me*?

Talk about pressure…

Not only that, but if he knows all about me the same way I do him, he has to be aware that I'm no virgin.

I pause just outside of my bedroom. "You know that I—"

Sammael turns into me, cutting me off with one look.

"I am your mate as you are mine." He lifts the hand I'm not holding, trailing the side of his shadowy claw down the edge of my jaw. "Not that human male's. Not any other male's, either."

Translation: no more 'dates' with my co-worker.

I'm okay with that. I like Jake. He's a sweet guy, and if I hadn't sent him home the other night, I'm sure we would've had some fun.

Sammael, though... I'm pretty sure it's going to be fun, but it'll be more than that, too.

And I can't wait.

The fact it doesn't bother him that he's not my first makes me even more ready to choose him. With another tug, I let him know that I'm done talking about that. That's my past... my new demon mate will be my future.

Once I've led him into my bedroom—the first time he's been inside with my conscious permission—I park him next to my bed before letting go of his hand.

"Hope..."

"Give me a sec, okay?"

"Of course."

Heading over to my dresser, I go rooting through my drawer, cursing under my breath.

"What is the matter, my Hope?"

"I thought I had some condoms in here," I mutter.

When I was half-crazed with lust thanks to the mate sickness—and I really was thinking about working it out with Jake—I told myself there were probably condoms left in there from Corey. Sure, that was two years ago and they might be out of date, but I'm a stickler on protection and I haven't been on birth control since we broke up.

Can demons and human mates even have kids? I don't know, but it doesn't matter. Condoms are a must since I don't want them.

Sammael moves next to me, so close I can feel the warmth of his skin. "Con-dom. Why do I get the image of some kind of sheath for my cock?"

Damn, that's sexy. The way he rumbled 'cock'... if I wasn't already turned on at just the thought of finally seeing what he has under those shadows of his, that would've done it.

Which is precisely why I need a condom.

"It is," I say, distracted, searching through my drawer again as though one might suddenly appear. "Protection for both of us. I guess, since you're immortal, you're not worried about diseases or anything, but... look. I'm okay with being your mate. That doesn't mean I want to get knocked up anytime soon."

"Knocked up?"

I shrug. "You know. Pregnant."

"Ah... Well, never worry. You will not."

I want to trust him, but I've heard something like that before. "Okay, but I might still have one in here—"

"You misunderstand, my mate. I cannot get you with spawn unless we mate on the night of the gold moon."

Wait... "Really?"

"Check my essence."

I don't really want to risk another headache when I have my heart set on climbing into bed with Sammael, but this is too important to just take his word on.

Oh. He's right. The gold moon serves as the deadline for any mates to finalize that promise thing I made when I read the spell—which actually is a mating vow, so thanks to whoever thought it was a good idea to write 'promise' and not 'you're signing your life away here'—but after the initial claiming, if a pair of demon mates fuck on the night of the gold moon, they're pregnant.

Fuck any other day, you're fine. The gold moon? *Boom*. Babies.

No, thanks.

Good thing that tonight's not the gold moon in Sombra, either. I really want to do this with him now, but not if I'm going to end up with a baby after it.

Sammael is a virgin. I wasn't worried about diseases, just a little Hope junior. So, since I won't be needing a condom after all, I shut the drawer, then reach down for the hem of my shirt, about to remove it.

Sammael stops me by clearing his throat.

I glance over at him.

"Are you certain, my mate? Once bonded, there is no changing our minds. Our tie will be forever."

Forever...

Geez, Sammael, do you have to sell this any harder? I'm already sold.

"Am I sure that I want to do this? Yeah. I am." Unless it's not me who's having cold feet here. I finger the edge of my shirt, catching his eye. "What about you? You ready to do this?"

"More than you know," he rumbles.

Okay, then.

That clear, I start to yank up my shirt, pausing again halfway when Sammael lifts his hand up.

"Allow me."

He waves—and I gasp.

One second, I'm fully dressed. The next? I don't have a stitch of clothes on me.

Not gonna lie. That *is* pretty cool. Glancing down at my tits, I marvel at how he could have done that.

Magic? It has to be magic.

"Okay, wow." I chuckle in ill-disguised delight. "That can definitely come in handy on those lazy mornings when I just don't feel like getting undressed."

I don't think he heard my tease. When he doesn't

say anything in response, I lift my gaze and it's easy to see why: he's way too busy gazing at my naked body, stunned by its appearance.

A lump lodges in my throat, good humor suddenly slapped aside by nerves.

Does he not like what he sees?

He saw me naked before. In my dreams... he touched me and he licked me, and he already knew exactly what I looked like... but this is different, isn't it?

I swallow roughly. "Sammael?"

"Beautiful," he murmurs in Sombran.

I give a start. That wasn't English. The word is different, a harsher syllable that ends in a hiss, but I know exactly what it means.

Huh. I guess I can understand his demon language now. Another perk of being mates and doing that essence exchange thing?

That would explain how he went from knowing a 'little' English to being fluent after I touched him. Thanks to his essence, I can translate Sombran into English instantly, with only the slightest accent to his voice to tell me that he's switched to his language from of mine.

Awesome. That's something else that has me amazed, but as Sammael waves his hand again, removing his shadows so that I get my first peek at his full-blown erection, I'm a little distracted by something even more fascinating.

Like the rest of him, his dick is red. The crown is a deeper shade, more purple than anything, and there isn't a single strand of hair on his groin which only makes it clear just how big he is.

I gulp and point. "That might be a problem."

He looks down, cupping his balls before running his fingers along the underside of his shaft.

The fact that it takes him a while to go from root to tip makes me even more apprehensive.

Logically, I knew he was so much bigger than me. His dick is perfectly in proportion to his size... but still. I'm human. I might be his fated mate, and he obviously believes that means we'll fit... yeah. A banana being shoved into a hole the size of a penny.

I'm not so sure it's going to work.

"Do you trust me?" Sammael asks.

"As much as I can trust anyone, sure."

He dips his head, pressing his lips against mine. Remembering our lessons, he deepens the kiss until I'm reaching out, digging my fingers into his chest.

Pulling back, his breath soft and warm on my face, he says, "For now, I will accept that response, but I will not rest until you trust me more than anyone you have ever known."

"Okay," I breathe out, lost in his purple eyes.

Reaching down, gripping me by my naked waist the same way he did in my dreams, Sammael lifts me up easily, then lays me out in the middle of the bed.

With that thick cock of his leading the way, he joins me.

His gaze is locked on my pussy as he guides me to spread my legs wide open to him. For a heartbeat, I think he's going to give up on going straight for penetrative sex and do oral instead, but this tie between us... this growing bond? It's telling me that my demon mate is so desperate to finalize it that, as hungry as he is for my taste, he wants forever with me more.

And that means he needs to fuck me, spilling his come inside of me.

It won't last long. He's a nine-hundred-year-old virgin who knows he gets to keep me once I'm full of his jizz. Even if he had the stamina to bang me all night long, I can sense... I don't know... it's like his goal is to make me feel good so I enjoy him and his touch, then mark me so that I really am his bonded mate.

I guess, on the plus side, it's a good thing we'll have forever then...

Now, I'm expecting a little discomfort as he climbs over me, nudging my entrance with the blunt yet noticeably hot head of his cock. I've been with guys of all sizes before, some thick and long, others short and fat, and one notable guy who was eight inches but so narrow, I felt like he was poking me with a pencil... but I'm bracing myself for Sammael.

There's a small amount of resistance, but I'm so slippery wet it doesn't do much; not even seeing that monster in real life did anything to dull my desire for him. Sammael holds his weight up on his arms, slowly pushing, and I expect him to maybe get the tip in.

Will that be enough for us to be bonded?

I freaking hope so.

But something really weird happens. He keeps pushing, going slowly, but there's no denying that he's still fitting more and more of himself inside of me. I don't get it. It's been two years since I've had sex with anything other than my vibe, and that thing is nowhere as thick as Sammael is. I know a girl can stretch, too, but damn.

I'm panting. I feel full. Stuffed, even. As he pushes, he's hitting nerve endings I didn't even know I had... but when he finally bottoms out, I'm staring up at him in wonder.

"I am shadow," is his explanation before, slowly, slowly, he begins to withdraw.

"I... *huh*?"

"Shadow," he repeats. "I can adjust the size of my cock by turning just that part of my body to shadow. Then, with the edge of it more insubstantial than my solid form, I can fill you perfectly."

'Perfectly' isn't the word for it.

Now that I'm no longer apprehensive about what he's packing, I start to move a little with him. Before long, Sammael develops a rhythm of his own, fucking me gently at first before moving faster, rocking his hips quickly. I already figured it would be a race for him to nut inside of me, and I don't hold it against him.

Honestly, I want to be able to claim him as my mate, too.

Of course, that means I have to give him a little help.

Reaching between our bodies, I start rubbing my clit furiously so that, when Sammael finally bucks up into me, roaring his release, I'm right there with him.

I start panting his name, clutching whatever part of his big body that I can, clinging to him as though part of me thinks he'll vanish like the rest of my dreams do... until a bond snaps into place between us, tying me to Sammael in a way I recognize instinctively.

Because he was right, wasn't he? I'm his one true mate—and he's *mine*.

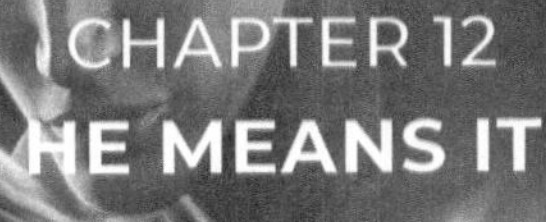

HOPE

All along, I thought of the essence exchange between Sammael and me as some kind of cheat code. Like it's a download where he plugged everything about himself into me, and I did the same for him.

I'm only twenty-eight and I haven't lived what you would call an overly exciting life. It's no surprise that he finds it a lot easier to absorb and digest details about mine. Sammael, I've learned from my quick foray into his memories, isn't just a mage. He's also a soldier who spent close to eight centuries—*eight centuries*—serving under the ruler of his world.

He's seen a lot of shit during that time. Done a lot, too. Since I'm the only mate he'll ever have, my experience in bed seems like the only thing I have on him. Luckily, that doesn't seem to bother him. He understands that humans don't have a fated mate like Sombra demons do. We can *be* one, and now that I've bonded myself to him, he's going to be it for me forever—the bond finalizing between us will make it that way, plus that little gift of immortality I got when I fucked him—but we both have a past.

It's just... different ones.

But that's my point. I'm not even thirty and my new mate is over *nine hundred years* old. To an immortal demon, the years don't really matter. So long as we're both 'mature', he thinks that we're of a similar age. Maybe we are, but that doesn't change the fact that he has thirty times the years I've seen—and more than thirty times the experiences I've had, either.

He gave me his essence right before he asked me to be his forever mate. It took me a few seconds to process that and use my overall reaction to him basically being downloaded into my mind to decide that, if Fate was willing to give me a devoted guy who loved me so much, he found me in another world and followed me into my *dreams*, she can't be wrong.

So far, I'm pretty solid on my decision. There's no take-backs or anything, so it's a good thing that I wake up the next morning without any regrets so far...

In fact, I feel pretty freaking good. Sammael has me tucked against his naked body, keeping me warm and cozy, his thick black hair mingling with my much shorter bob as I use the strands as a cushion against my pillow.

My hand is sprawled out on his chest. I'd fallen asleep lying there after my last orgasm, too dozed and sated to even get up and clean myself. I tried, but Sammael nuzzled my neck, his shadowy claws gripping my waist gently as though afraid I was going to leave him once we both finished.

Clinging to me, such love and affection and gratitude rushing down our finalized bond, hitting me in my heart... I couldn't find it in me to disentangle my body from his. Murmuring my name in his husky voice, I let him talk me into staying right where I was.

I must have shifted in my sleep, though. I'm curled up against him instead of on top of him, one leg thrown over his tree trunk of a thigh.

He's in his solid, red-skinned form. Fast asleep, his chest rises and falls under my hand as I snuggle closer. I'm awake, though I can't see any reason why I shouldn't enjoy this peaceful moment with my demon since I don't have work today. And that's just what I'm about to do when the early morning chill hits my exposed back and I scoot a little closer to Sammael, trying to steal as much of his warmth as I can.

We're both still naked from last night. Sammael must have grabbed my blanket and covered us up with it after I knocked out—or I grabbed it in my sleep like I usually do—because it's pulled up to my tits and that's about all. I need him to warm me up some more and I keep going until I'm basically wrapped around him like a spider monkey.

And that's when I realize that, just because his essence allows me to use him like Google, asking a question and getting an answer almost immediately, I don't just *know* everything. I have to ask the question first—and it never occurred to me to wonder if demons get morning wood.

Welp. I can answer that one now. As I lift my knee, moving my hip so I can get even closer to Sammael, my thigh bumps into the obvious erection he has.

Suddenly more awake than I was before, I glance down. I noticed the blanket before when I woke up sleepily, looking over at my new mate with half-closed eyes, but it isn't until I blink a few times and stare that I see it's tented.

And, yeah... even with the blanket covering it, that monstrous cock is even bigger in the dawning sunlight.

Sliding my hand down his sculpted chest, fingers gliding past a set of abs that would make any body-builder jealous, I don't stop until I've found his hairless groin. I tap the base of his cock, itching to grab him and play.

Last night, Sammael told me I could touch him where I wanted, how I wanted, *when* I wanted. He reaffirmed the mating promise that made us bonded mates, vowing that his heart and his body belong to me.

In that case…

Shifting my position so that both of my legs are on one side of Sammael, I wrap one hand around his bicep, then take a firm hold of his cock. I start out by stroking it gently before increasing my pace, grinning to myself when his body jerks and, suddenly, I'm gazing into a pair of heavy-lidded purple eyes.

"Hope?"

My name is swallowed by a grunt as he moves to his side, giving me easier access to his dick. If I had any doubt that he wouldn't consent to being woken up with my hands on his junk, they're immediately dashed when he starts thrusting gently into my fist.

"Good morning, Sammael."

Breathing heavily as I stroke him, he slides his hand beneath my head, cradling it, then says, "You may call me 'Sam' if you would like."

Um. Okay. Not what I thought he would say when I woke him up to the beginnings of a handjob, but maybe that's because he's still trying to make me feel comfortable with him.

What an adorable demon. He fucked me within an inch of my life last night, claiming me and promising to keep me forever, and he still thinks that he might scare me off. He has my essence. I'm a chickenshit when it comes to ridiculous things, but now that I know I'm not crazy—that, while he was a phantom, he really *did* haunt me, dragging that book everywhere so that I'd read it—and I've gotten used to his looks, I'm not scared of him.

He brought me acorns because, after watching Peter give Wendy one, he thought it was a kiss. How the hell could I be scared of a guy who did that, monster or not?

Still, that doesn't change the fact that he isn't human. To me, 'Sammael' is a demon. 'Sam' is the demon hunter on that old CW show I watched when I was in high school.

Shoot, one of the best things about my new mate is that he *isn't* human.

"I'll stick with 'Sammael' for now, if that's all the same to you."

"Of course. Whatever you wish, my mate."

Whatever I wish, huh?

I tighten my grip on his cock. My fingers don't quite touch, but I squeeze as I stroke, making sure he knows exactly what I'm thinking.

His eyes close—hiding the purple glow—as he throws his head back against the pillow beneath him. His horns jab up into the air as he bucks his hips, pushing his erection into my palm. The heat of his flesh becomes impossibly warmer as his balls slap into the side of my hand, and it's *delicious*.

It also leaves me wanting more.

"Did you mean it?" I ask him.

It takes Sammael a moment to realize I said something. "What is that, my mate?"

I squeeze him. "I said, did you mean it?"

His face screws up, lips parting as his breath comes out in a frantic pant as he obviously chases his orgasm. "Mean what?"

"That your heart is mine?" I ask, rubbing my thumb over the sensitive crown of his cock. "That your body is, too?"

Last night, he did. His essence confirms that he's thought of me as his from the moment he read the true love spell himself, but... I don't know... something about this moment has me needing to hear it for myself again.

"Yes." It's a gasp as he reaches out, running the side of his thumb along the height of my cheek. "*Always.*"

Good.

Smiling over at him, I let go of his cock.

Sammael's expression goes from bliss to confusion in an instant. It softens when he sees my smile, and when I push on his shoulder, showing him I want him on his back, he doesn't hesitate to do what I want.

And then, watching him closely as my grin widens, I do what *I* want.

Last night, Sammael mated me in missionary. That seems to be the way that most demons fuck, allowing the much larger male to dominate his demoness in the bedroom. And as much as I enjoy having a guy cover me the way that Sammael did, I decide to give him a little hint about what it's like to have a human chick as a mate.

I'm not as intimidated about his size as I was before. Now I know that, even if we don't seem to fit right away, he can control his size until he fills me up perfectly. So, throwing one leg over his hip, straddling my demon, I grab his cock again, positioning it so that I sink right down on top of him.

He's speechless as I slip his cock inside of me, murmuring softly when I brace myself by placing both of my hands on his chest before letting gravity take over.

Only then, when I'm fully seated on him, completely full and with only a tiny pinch to tell me that he's stretching me out even more than he had last night, do I move my hands from his pecs to his shoulders.

I bend, urging him to take one of my tits in his hand. He does without a question, keeping his claws shadowy so that he doesn't stab me there as he begins to massage my boob before bending his head, darting his heated tongue out to swipe at my nipple before he latches on.

Yes.

This is Sammael tapping into my essence, isn't it? I've always had a thing about my lovers playing with my tits, and nothing gets me off faster than a guy taking deep pulls off one like he's trying to milk me. It's just a kink of mine, even though there's no chance I'll ever breastfeed, but it drives me crazy.

I don't know what exactly Sammael likes just yet, but as I start to ride him, from the way he reacts, lifting his hips to buck up into me anytime he thinks I'm about to climb off of him again… cowgirl might be at the top of his list.

He releases my boob with a soft sucking sound, then says, "I didn't know that mating could be like this."

I roll my hips, pleasure fueling me as he gasps, fingers going right to my waist to keep me with him. "Isn't that why you spent all that time searching for yours?"

"I longed for my mate because I wanted my soul to feel complete," he says, so seriously that I stop riding him for a moment. "I wanted the one female who would spend the rest of her existence together with me. To love her and protect her. To love and protect *you*, my beloved. To be the male worthy of you, my Hope."

A lump lodges in my throat. I honestly thought it was all about sex for him… but it isn't, is it? The bond made it seem like it was—the mate sickness, too—but Sammael… again, I can tell he means it.

Swallowing roughly, intimately aware that his

massive cock is lodged completely inside of me, I start to move again.

"You will," I murmur as he picks up his pace, angling his hips just so that I'm bumping my clit against his groin every time I shift my weight again. Pleasure is about to crash into me like a wave, his taut body a sure sign that my demon is right there with me.

Dropping my head, I press an open-mouthed kiss on his chest as I tell him, "You are, Sammael."

I just hope that I'm the woman worthy of his devotion...

AN HOUR LATER, I FINALLY CRAWL OUT OF THE BED. Sammael seems hesitant to let me, but when I admit that I need to *go*, he places his big hand gently on the back of my neck, holding me in place so that he can give me a kiss.

He's gotten so much better already. I barely notice his fangs as he sucks my bottom lip into the heat of his mouth before nuzzling my temple with his chin.

I get the feeling he's scent marking me or something, but since I'm full of his come and his body touched almost every inch of mine between last night and this morning, it's pointless. I probably smell more like Sammael than I do Hope right now.

And I kinda like it.

He told me that I smell delicious, but something about the way Sammael smells like fire reminds me of camping with my mom and Jo when we were both Girl Scouts. It's not an unpleasant smell, and the nostalgia that comes with it only makes me feel a little guilty that my sister will never get to know Sammael.

My mom, too, of course, but Johanna is still here with us. She actually *saw* Sammael—and then promptly had her memories of him erased because humans aren't supposed to know that demons exist.

Unless you're the mate to one, of course...

I think about hopping in the shower real quick, then change my mind. I do brush my teeth, marveling over how Sammael didn't even mention my morning breath—or have any himself—before doing a quick clean-up after I pee. Then, feeling a little more human, I shuffle back into my bedroom just as my empty stomach starts to growl.

I haven't had anything to eat since Johanna brought pizza with her last night. And Sammael... he hasn't had anything to eat in a while, has he?

He's sitting up in my bed, blankets pooled around his waist as he uses a claw to thumb through one of the romance books he must have grabbed down from my shelf. From his awed expression as he reads it, he seems to enjoy it, though maybe he's getting some ideas from the spicy scenes.

The thought of getting to act out some of my

favorites with my new mate makes me smile—and turns me on more than it probably should. It's a good thing he's covered again because I'm not so sure I can control myself around him right now, and we should probably go ahead and have breakfast.

Hovering in the doorway, keeping a little distance from my tempting demon, I ask him, "Are you hungry?"

His eyes brighten, a look of surprise flashing across his face as though it never occurred to him that he should be.

When he was a ghost, he didn't need to eat or pee or even sleep. That last one isn't so unusual for a Sombra demon, his download tells me, but a big guy like Sammael? He needs a lot of calories to support both of his forms as well as the magic his type of demon has.

Not to mention the fact that he definitely burned through plenty last night and this morning. If my stomach is growling, ready for some sustenance after our workout, I can only imagine how ravenous he is.

"I am," Sammael tells me, setting the book down on my nightstand. "But I hunger more for your cunt than I do meat."

Oh.

Oh.

I guess I'm not the only one who still has sex on the brain.

Screw it. Breakfast can wait.

Instead of grabbing some clothes so that I'm not walking around my kitchen butt-naked, I saunter off to my bed, delighting in his unblinking stare as he watches every single sway of my hip, every bounce of my bare tits.

Sammael's eyes shine brightly as I approach, fisting the blanket and tossing it away from him.

Holy shit. I thought I milked every drop from him, but his cock is so hard again, it looks like it might poke my eye out if I let it.

Good thing I have a little practice with this.

Climbing onto my bed, I crawl on all fours until I've moved my body between his legs. He just about stops breathing, almost as though he can't believe that I would even think about doing what I'm totally going to do... but he does widen his legs to give me some room to maneuver closer to him.

"Are you sure?" I tease, moving into my new mate. "Because I'm thinking I can do with a little meat myself."

I don't know if it's my last couple of years of celibacy talking, the lingering effects from the mate sickness, or maybe even a honeymoon period between two mates, but despite already getting off once this morning with him, I'm just as ready as he is to do it again.

But, after a quick poke and prod at his essence, I

find out that some demonesses in Sombra do honor their mates by worshiping their cock. Not because it will help with any kind of procreation, but because they love their males enough to give them pleasure with their mouths.

Here, it's just a BJ. To Sammael, sucking him off will show him that I consider him my mate.

And, well, he is, isn't he?

As I duck my head, dabbing my tongue along the crown of his cock, Sammael digs his claws into my sheets. I hear them tear, the big demon losing enough control from that one, single lick to forget to turn them to shadow. He immediately starts to apologize, but I cut him off by taking the entire bulbous head between my lips.

Sammael strangles his apologies, just like I wanted him to do.

Hollowing my cheeks, sucking him like he's my favorite flavor of lollipop, I swirl my tongue around the tip before peering up at him through the fringe of my eyelashes. I suck again, then let his slick cock slip free from my mouth for a moment.

"Forget the sheets," I tell him. "I got 'em for ten bucks at Target. I can get more. Do whatever makes you feel good, okay? I want you to enjoy this."

After all, it's his first time. Our mating might have been a little clumsy, and he didn't last half as long last night as he did this morning, but that... that charms me. I haven't been with a virgin guy since I hooked up with Tanner Gordon the first time when were both sixteen and clueless together, but there's something... something *sweet* about sex with my demon.

It's the affection I see in his face, and the way he strokes my hair as though I'm precious. Thanks to his long arms, he can reach the back of my head without shifting from his position, but he doesn't guide me back to his cock or try to fuck my mouth. Instead, he pets me, almost like he's saying 'thank you' as I go down on him again.

He's too big, too thick for me to take more than a few inches of his cock, but that's enough for him. Adding my hands into the act, fisting him with both of them, using my saliva and his pre-come to stroke him off in turn as I lick and suck and nuzzle the crown, I keep going until Sammael gasps and, with another pained whisper of my name, fills my mouth with spunk that's so warm, it goes down like salty coffee when I swallow it.

Unexpected, but fuck if that wasn't one of the sexiest damn things I've ever experienced in my life.

And I get to look forward to forever with him?

Wow.

CHAPTER 13

CHAINS

SAMMAEL

I think I always suspected that forever with my mate would not last very long at all.

As Hope pulls on her coverings, I watch from my post in her bed as though this glimpse of her delectable mortal body is the last I'll have. I savor the scrap of silk traveling up her legs, hiding her soft cunt from my view. I do the same when she binds her breasts before pulling on a piece that covers her completely on top, then another for her bottom. I know from her essence that they're her favored 'sweats', and what she usually wears when she is staying in her quarters instead of going to her library.

I also understand why she spends all of her time surrounded by books. She loves them, but tending to them is her way of earning the coin that all humans need to possess in their realm. There is no barter system or trades like we have in Sombra, and my Hope must purchase her food rather than hunt it.

I am her male. Her *mate*. There is no way for me to earn coin myself without breaking the duke's first law, so I would provide for her in other ways. I shall give her pleasure, then gratefully eat the meals she creates. I shall make it so that her jingly bits of metals—her keys—and her foot coverings—her slippers—do not get lost, and she will bring happiness to my life just by existing.

A perfect pair we are. I have my magic returned now, and once I understand all of her needs, I will use my powers to conjure her whatever her heart desires. I will strive to prove myself to her for as long as I can—

—but, to my deepest regrets, it is nowhere near long enough.

My one relief is that Hope is not in her private quarters when the portal into Sombra suddenly appears. After covering herself, she has gone downstairs in search of the morning meal she calls 'breakfast', and I am lying in her bedding, enjoying the sweet scent of her cunt and my seed mingling together that fills the space.

It has barely been an entire human day since Hope summoned me and, after completing the essence exchange, accepted me as her mate. I should be grateful that Duke Haures gave me that much time. The ruler of Sombra, he has the ability to sense whenever a portal off-plane opens, and I've always suspected that his unique brand of magic would also tell him when the *verus amor* spell summoned one of his subjects to the human world.

My portal here opened more than four cycles ago. As a phantom, Duke Haures couldn't send any of his guards to find me since it was as though I no longer existed. From the moment Hope fixed that—fixed *me* —he must have bided his time, waiting to send his soldiers after me for my crimes.

I have done the same for him many times. Usually, the first visit is a warning unless the demon has already broken the duke's decrees. With Malphas, Glaine and I visited him on Earth to remind him that he must bond his human mate to him before the next golden moon or it would be chains for him.

All Sombra demons know when the gold moon occurs in our realm, whether we're on that plane or not. We just passed the second since I left my home, but now that I've claimed Hope as mine, there is no worry that the gold moon serves as a deadline for our mating.

But that's not why the familiar pair of males are emerging from the portal, stepping from the shadows of Sombra into the sanctity of Hope's private quarters, is it?

Glaine steps out first. He's firmly in his shadow form, all inky blank with the edges of his shadows wavering as he steps forward, his blazing green eyes finding me in Hope's bedding.

I match him. If he's choosing to be shadow, I do the same as I move so that I'm standing, facing off against my fellow guard.

Especially since Loki is also wearing his shadows.

I don't know him as well as I do Glaine. For centuries, he was my pupil, but then he stole the matefinder spell and spent a full century in the shadows on the edge of Sombra. He lost control and lost his essence, his purple eyes turning white as he went demonic, and though he's changed—his human mate bringing him back from the brink—he is not the male I once knew in the School of Mages.

I recognize him, though, even in his shadows. The outline of his double pair of horns makes it obvious who he is, as well as the deep purple shade of his eyes and the tense way he carries his bulk as though prepared to turn solid and ram into me at a moment's notice.

For so many centuries, I was the mage who built the portals that carried Glaine off-plane to do Duke Haures's bidding. Since I vanished, it seems as though Loki took my place.

He says nothing as he drifts behind Glaine, leaving the guard to take point.

Glaine meets my gaze. "Where is the book?"

I'm not surprised he asks. Deep down, I knew that —when they came for me... and they *would* come for me—it would be because of the *Grimoire du Sombra* I stole.

Where is it? It's downstairs where Hope left it before we made our way to her quarters. I don't tell Glaine that, though, since he would go and retrieve it —and I do not want Hope to know he is here.

So I tell him, "It is with my mate," because it's the truth, and all I'm willing to offer my old friend.

He nods, accepting that. Then, his nostrils flaring, he must confirm that Hope is my *bonded* mate from our mingled scents in the room because Glaine's eyes glare, a bright green shade similar to that I've seen on the streets outside of Hope's home.

"You have made her yours so soon," he says.

"She is my bonded mate."

Loki and Glaine exchange a look. The younger demon shakes his head, showing off his two-horns, while Glaine's scowl deepens.

"We were supposed to retrieve you before you claimed your mate," he explains. "I was led to believe that humans tend to make their demons wait until closer to the gold moon. That there would be enough time to settle this before you involved the mortal."

Some of the humans might have. Not my Hope.

She is not quite a mortal anymore, either. Now that

I've given her my essence and my seed, she is as immortal as I am. Her human lifespan is now unending, just as though she was born a demoness, and even if something happens to me, she will live on... until she chooses not to, that is.

I have not had the chance to explain that to her yet. From my essence, she would know that, but she's only had access to it for such a small amount of time. So, while my mate understands the concept of 'forever', there are details that she still needs to learn.

No time. As Loki lifts his shadowed hands, already conjuring at a nod from Glaine, I accept that this is no warning. Glaine is not here to remind me that I must bond my Hope to me before the gold moon. I already did, and Loki continues to wield magic, building the links of golden chain between his palms.

It is for me. That's why he is here. So long as Loki uses his mage abilities to summon a portal and keep it open for Glaine, he had no reason to follow the guard off-plane. But Glaine cannot conjure chains... and Loki can.

As he finishes his cast, ending the chain with gold cuffs that will fit on my wrists, Loki says to Glaine, "Should we bring her back to Mavro with us?"

I will accept the chains if that is to be my fate. I refuse to see my mate wearing them, too.

"You cannot—"

"Duke Haures trusted you," Glaine says, cutting me off with a pointed reminder.

I trust you...

I struggle to contain my temper. If he believes me a traitor, Glaine will see Hope in chains just to spite me. I won't let him do that if I can. "I know that."

"And you betrayed him."

Glaine doesn't ask me why. He *knows* why.

And, given the chance, he would do the same... though that doesn't change a thing about what he's come to the human realm to do this morning.

Every Sombran demon longs for their female. I believed I was owed a mate more than most. A powerful mage... it was my reward after a lifetime in service to Duke Haures.

I found her, too, but Hope... she only just learned of me. She agreed to be my mate, believing we have an eternity to be together because I was too afraid to tell her that the duke would eventually send his soldiers after me.

She will know after. When she returns to her quarters and I am gone, she will be able to learn the truth through my essence. Our bond will weaken—though, as far as I am aware, it should not break—and, through the veil, I don't know if I will be able to sense her any longer, but at least she will discover that her male...

Her male...

Her male was never worthy of her.

"Take me." I hold out my wrists to Loki. "Give me the chains, but promise me you will not go after my Hope."

"She is your bonded mate, but with you in the dungeons, will she have your loyalty? I think we should bring her to the duke."

No!

"Leave her," I snarl. In response to my temper, Loki immediately sends the chains at me. I ignore them, though they're a reminder that I must not fight back for Hope's sake. Swallowing my pride, I soften my voice and tell Glaine, "I will make her forget me. Forget Sombra. I'll go with you, but only if you leave my mate be."

I was once the most powerful mage in all of Sombra. I lost my magic for a time to be with Hope, and just when I thought I had them both, I will have neither.

Powerful... am I powerful enough to let her go?

It is a simple spell to pluck the memory of me and everything she knows about Sombra from her. She would have my essence, but no knowledge of how to use it, and she would continue to exist until, one day, she was gone because she didn't know she could exist forever.

And when I hear a soft gasping sound from the entrance to her quarters, seeing Hope with her eyes wide and her mouth slightly parted, showing off her small, human teeth... I wish I could do the same to my own memories because I never want to remember the look of hurt that flashes across her face when she heard how I offered to give her up.

I want to tell her that I'm doing it for her. Before I can get the words out, though, her accusing stare drops to the chains on my wrists before she spots Glaine and Loki, standing apart from the rest of the shadows in her space.

"What is going on here? Sammael? Are these your friends? What are they doing here? Why... why are you wearing *chains*?"

"Hope." The heavy chains rattle as my hands shake. "You should go back downstairs."

"What? Leave you? No way. And you're not going anywhere, either."

As much as I don't want to leave her, I also didn't want her to see me like this. She would understand that I was taken prisoner by the duke's guards, but I would much rather she never see me in my chains.

Especially since I will do anything to keep her from being clapped in a pair of her own.

We're bonded. As mates, she is allowed to know of Sombra—but maybe it would be a kindness to help her forget.

Glaine is the only one here that doesn't understand the human tongue. Hope, in her panic, reverted to her language which has the other demon frowning.

"What is she saying?"

Loki translates. "She wants to know why we are here. I don't think she understands how Sammael was able to summon her... or why we have him in chains."

"Then maybe we should give her her own pair and bring her back to Sombra with us like I thought."

Hope gasps. Glaine doesn't know English, but Hope? With my essence, she can understand *him*.

Put her in chains? *Never*.

The cuffs aren't completely sealed. I can still access my magic. I could erase myself from Hope's heart, knowing she will always have mine.

I lift my hands... and then I do nothing but wait for a few moments before I turn to Loki and tell him, "There. Now seal the chains, Loki. Glaine, I am ready to face the duke. But you must promise to leave Hope to her human world."

Glaine hesitates for a moment, then he nods.

Loki moves forward, waving his hands over the cuffs. The moment he seals them, it's like someone has put a damper on my bond. Hope is closed off from me, leaving only a trace of her essence to keep me company.

The way she stumbles forward, I'm sure she feels the same—and she doesn't understand it. That's the last emotional burst I received from my mate: confusion, followed by a determination to rescue me from my fate.

"Sammael?" Hope looks from me to Glaine and Loki, then back. "What? No!"

My heart aches, but I will do anything to keep my mate safe.

Anything, except allow her to forget me.

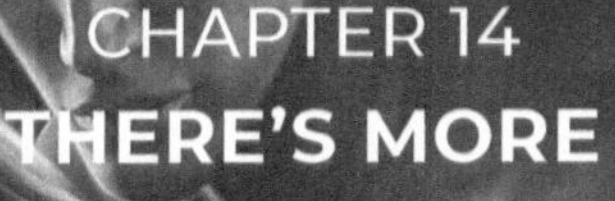

HOPE

He's gone.

I only just got to know Sammael, and he's *gone*.

The shadowy figure with the scowl and the glowing green eyes nudged him in the back and, with one last forlorn look over at me, he allowed the flickering flames in that big hole to swallow him up.

I guess I should be grateful that he changed his mind about erasing himself from my memories the same way he did to Jo, but maybe it would have been preferable to the way my heart aches to know that I only just found him and now I've lost him because... because...

Fuck! I don't even know why they took Sammael. I

was downstairs, finishing up breakfast when I felt like I had the wind knocked out of me. Leaning against the counter, spatula in one hand, my other clutching my chest through my sweatshirt, it took me a moment to realize that I wasn't having a sudden heart attack. It was painful and unexpected, and once I got past the shock of it, I couldn't shake the feeling that something was wrong.

That the pain came from this new bond I shared with my mate.

I didn't even bother turning the stove off. With the bacon still crackling away behind me, I tossed the spatula on the counter, then bolted for the stairs.

The whole time I dashed up to the second floor, I hoped that I would find Sammael taking up most of my bed like before. My blowjob skills did wonders to convince him to stay back and relax while I went down to the kitchen to whip up a meal. I had to. When we finally got back to talking about if we were hungry or not and I asked him what they ate in Sombra, the image of a fuzzy part squirrel, part house cat with a shadowy build and glowing white eyes popped into my brain.

No, thanks. I don't know what that was supposed to be, but I told him I would introduce him to human food. So I'm not the world's best cook. I can still make a mean bacon and eggs, and since Sammael doesn't have anything else to compare it to, I figured it would be a win.

Only... when I forced myself to slow down so that I don't freak him out with my tendency to think the worst and overreact, I walked into my room to see that he wasn't alone.

There were two other Sombra demons in my bedroom, who were staring off against my mate before I showed up and they turned in unison to face me. Behind the bigger of the two—who had purple eyes like Sammael and *two* pairs of horns jutting from his head—I saw... something.

I didn't know what it was at first. It looked like a big oval-shaped hole about the size of my closet door. The edges of it were hazy, similar to one of the demon's ink-black outlines, while the inside... I swear to God... was full of *fire.*

Through the flames, I saw a world with red earth, black trees, a large moon, and enough heat wafting off of it that it warmed up my entire room. Compared to the morning chill, the heat was oppressive and thick, though none of the other demons seemed to notice that.

Me? I nearly choked on it—though there's a good chance it's more the surprise I experienced walking in on this scene than anything else.

Because Sammael... not only was he facing off against

the other two, but in the time since I went downstairs before coming back up to check on him, he got put in a pair of gleaming golden chains, complete with a heavy-looking cuff on each wrist that kept the links connected.

Then, after telling the scowling one that he was willing to take my memories, he had the other one seal the cuffs and that was it. He was gone, leaving the portal thing and the demon with the double set of horns to watch me closely as I don't know whether to cry, faint, or leap forward and jump after him.

I'm stunned. That's for sure. Being with Sammael was like a high, but as soon as those cuffs *clinked* shut, it was almost as though someone took that tie between us and looped it into a damn knot. I couldn't reach him even before he disappeared, and it takes me a second to understand that that... all of that... just happened.

I remember it all. Not one second of the last few days is missing from my memory which is saying something since it's usually such shit.

Shaking off my stupor, I finally react. Rushing forward, I shout his name.

That was my mistake.

He obviously wanted the other demons to think that he was going to make me forget all about him and Sombra. I don't know why they came for him—nothing in his essence makes me think that he's a bad guy, or a demon on the run—but I do instinctively understand the chains.

He's a prisoner.

Of the duke he used to work for?

Most likely.

Do I know why?

Not even a little. Honestly, I don't really care, either. That's the best thing about an essence exchange, I guess. I know every inch of Sammael's soul intimately, the same way I was able to discover his body. If he was, like, a demon murderer or something, I'd know. If he was lying… if telling me that he was my mate just so I'd fuck him was a cruel lie, I'd *know*.

This is one of the first times in my life where my anxiety isn't putting bad thoughts in my brain. The old Hope would easily believe I'd been duped.

The Hope that impulsively promised herself to Sammael?

If the purple-eyed demon—*Loki*—hadn't shifted his shadowy bulk to stand in front of the portal to stop me, I would've hopped in right after my demon, grabbing him by the chains to drag him back to Earth myself.

There isn't anything I wouldn't do for those I love. I might have only just gotten to know Sammael, but it doesn't matter. Fate gave him to me.

I want him back.

Though Loki is a shadow, I bounce right off of him. I wasn't expecting him to block me, he wasn't expecting me to bum rush him, and the result was that

I slammed into his billowy chest, hitting the solid layer beneath the shadows before falling backward on my ass.

It stings, but I shake it off. As quickly as I can, I hurry to my feet.

"Move," I tell him.

I'm so pissed, I use English. I noticed one of the two demons obviously had no idea what I was saying when I spoke before, but I guess it wasn't this one because he actually answers me in the same language.

"I cannot, Sammael's female."

His voice is more stilted than Sammael's. My demon has an obvious American accent, due to my download and the massive amounts of television he watched these last couple of months, teaching him my language. Loki? He says each word carefully, and though he knows English, I get the idea that it's not a language he uses often.

Oh, well.

"Yes, you can. It's real easy. You go over there and I..." What? Burn myself to a crisp in the flames?

I'm not a demon. I'm human. Would it even work for me?

As I'm hesitating, second-guessing my impulsivity, Loki shifts shapes. Instead of the shadowy demon hovering in front of the hole, he is more than seven feet of deep red demon, with a barrel chest, rich black hair that's nearly as long as Sammael's, those same double pair of horns only infinitely sharper now, and…

And…

I blink.

Is that a tattoo?

It is. It's written in a strange style, but the more I look at it, it's like I can translate, turning the letters into the English alphabet.

K…E…N—*Kennedy.*

Why does this demon have the name 'Kennedy' carved in his chest, set with a shimmery, silver ink that stands out on his red skin?

Mate, supplies a little voice in the back of his head. She's his mate.

I don't know about you, but 'Kennedy' doesn't seem like the sort of name that belongs to a demoness.

At least now I have a good idea how this demon knows my language…

Whatever. I don't care about that.

I point my finger at his chest. "You can't stop me." Loki totally can. "I have to go after him. He… that's my mate."

Loki's glowing purple eyes flare brightly before dimming again. "I warned him," he rumbles. "I warned him not to mess with the old magic. And now he's left you here on your own." The demon gnashes his fangs; surprisingly, he doesn't frighten me. "Gods damn it. He would have been better off making you forget him."

Yeah, well, maybe—but he didn't, and if he got to know me at all—from watching me as a ghost, or from my essence—then he had to expect I wouldn't just shrug and wave goodbye.

"He belongs to the duke now," is all he says before he glances behind him at the portal thing as if someone is calling him. He turns back, frowning as he quickly adds, "The book. You have the book?"

The book? The grimoire?

"I... yes, but—"

Loki takes a step back. "It will give you all the answers you need. Use it."

Use it? For what? "What?"

"You're not the only one," he grates out, using one of his thick claws to underline the tattoo on his chest.

Then, before I can ask him why that matters, he turns on his heel and walks right into the flames. An instant later, the portal winks out, leaving me standing alone in my bedroom with a rumpled bed, a thudding heart, and a stomach that's too twisted up for—

Breakfast.

Shit!

I smelled something burning while I was glaring at the demon. Part of me just assumed it was courtesy of the flames in the magic portal, but the moment it's gone, the stink of acrid, bitter, burnt bacon reaches me.

Shit, shit, shit!

I race downstairs, yipping when I see the plume of

faint grey smoke rising up over the ruined bacon. Turning the burner off, I toss the pan to the cool one next to it, wafting wildly before the smoke sets my alarm off.

Once I'm certain I'm not going to burn down my house, I leave the kitchen a mess, heading right for my living room. I have a pang in my chest when I notice the Ouija board still set up from last night. It gets worse when my bare feet tromp all over the sprinkled salt, tracking it even more across the floor as I head right for the spellbook.

It's open to the 'true love' spell. Thinking that's what Loki meant, I struggle through reading the manifest part, then the promise. It's even weirder that, when I'm on the second paragraph, the letters shift the same way the ones on Loki's chest did, turning from Sombran to English.

Even so, nothing freaking happens.

Okay. That would have been really nice if I could read the spell and bring Sammael back to me, but I doubted it would be that easy. There had to be a reason why the two demons bothered with putting chains on my mate, right? How much do I want to bet they'll prevent any magic use, either from Sammael or anyone trying to use it to summon him?

Flipping through the book, I check to see if there are any other spells that might do *something*.

I'm too frustrated to really look. All I keep thinking

about is that last look Sammael gave me, like he knew this separation was coming and that he was trying to memorize my face.

Screw that.

I grew up with a demanding older sister. We get along now, but I had to share everything I had with Johanna. My whole life, all I owned were hand-me-downs. Even when I got my first job at the mall when I was sixteen, I barely earned enough to get anything that wasn't from the thrift store.

I don't own my house. I rent. My car's a beater I bought online, third-hand by the time I got the title.

Sammael was finally something that's *mine*. No one else could have him, and as his one true mate, he wouldn't want any other.

And those demons *took* him from me.

I'll get him back. No matter what I have to do, I'll get him back... and, suddenly, I remember the last thing Loki said to me.

You're not the only one...

Hang on.

Kennedy.

Where have I seen that name before?

With a slap, I close the spellbook, then quickly flip open the inner cover.

That's right. There are *four* names written on the inside of the book: Susanna Benoit, Amy, Shannon Crewes, and Kennedy Barnes.

What if... what if that Kennedy and Loki's Kennedy are one and the same? If I'm not the only one... did Kennedy use the same book and summon her own Sombra demon mate? And the others? Shannon? Susanna? Amy's handwriting looks like it belongs to a little girl, but the rest look like they belong to adults.

And both Kennedy's and Shannon's seem fairly recent.

Phone. Where's my phone? Unless the women who left their names on this book are from a time before social media, there should be *some* trace of them online, right?

Humans aren't allowed to know about Sombra... but if they're a *mate*? That's a different story. And maybe... just maybe... if they know about Sombra, they might know how I can get my mate back.

It's worth a shot.

Upstairs, I remember. My phone is upstairs.

Leaving the book on my janky coffee table, I dash back upstairs. My stomach twists again when I remember that, less than half an hour ago, I was curled up with my demon.

Focus, Hope. Get your phone.

I do.

I can't stay up here right now. I just... I *can't.* Clutching my phone, I race down the stairs again, plopping down on my couch. As soon as my butt hits the cushion, I'm already opening up my phone and heading straight to Google.

"Kennedy... Kennedy... Kennedy Barnes. Okay. There's... crap. There's a lot." Social media profiles. Obituaries. Linkedin listings—

Wait.

"'Kennedy Barnes'," I read out loud, tapping the screen with my fingertip, excitement welling up inside of me, "'is the sole owner and proprietor of Turn the Page, a bookstore in Jericho, New York...'"

Dropping my phone to my lap, I grab the book and quickly turn it over. I stick my fingernail beneath the Westfield Library tag I slapped on the other day, peeling it up gently so that I can get a better look at the name of the store imprinted on the UPC sticker beneath it.

Normally, I pull the old stickers off, but for some reason I didn't when the grimoire was in the depository. Good thing, too, since, as soon as I ease it off, I see that I'm right.

Because this book once was sold at a bookstore with the very same name as Kennedy Barnes's: Turn the Page.

What are the freaking odds?

CHAPTER 15

SHANNON AND KENNEDY

HOPE

t was just before noon when I went downstairs to make us a late breakfast, early lunch.

By one o'clock, I have a plan.

Jericho, New York is pretty close to Westfield. Less than sixty miles away, I can make it there in about an hour and a half barring any traffic. The store is open until six o'clock, which gives me until two or three to get my shit together and head out.

I thought about calling the store, but I didn't. I couldn't. This is coming from the type of anxious mess who'd rather deal with a toothache for a week than call the dentist, or who pays extra to order my dinner online so that I don't have to talk to the restaurant on the phone.

Besides, what would I say? Humans aren't supposed to know about Sombra. If I find a mate and ask her, she might lie and pretend like she doesn't know what I'm talking about to keep the secret. No. I'm better off taking the ride and, if I find Kennedy, confronting her in person.

I'm nervous the entire drive, from the Garden State Parkway all the way up the LIE. There's more traffic than my phone first told me, and it ends up taking over *two* hours to get there. Luckily, it's still before six when I finally park and, anxiously strolling down Main Street, search for Turn the Page.

I smell the coffee on the wind and stumble upon a shop called The Beanery first. And maybe I'm stalling because I drove all this way and I'm terrified it'll end up having been pointless, but I think about ducking in to try out their pumpkin spice latte—and that's when I see the sign for Turn the Page right next door.

My heart is pounding. Half of me is insisting I should hop back in my car and forget this. Then I think about that last mournful gaze Sammael gave me, as though he was sure he was saying goodbye, and I get the nerve to grab the door handle.

It's a used book store with cramped shelves, paper-backs and hardcovers stacked all over the place, and that wonderful *old book* smell filling every corner. It immediately shouts 'cozy' to me, and if I wasn't here for a reason—and they weren't closing in less than an hour—I'd enjoy checking out each of the shelves.

Later, Hope. Maybe.

We'll see.

As far as I can tell, I'm the only person in the store except for the clerk behind the counter. She has her head bowed over a book when I walk in, glancing up when the bell over the door alerts her to my presence.

I'd put her about my age, maybe a couple of years older. She has a pretty face, open and friendly, with her long blonde hair pulled up in a high ponytail. Her eyes are a deep blue shade that pairs well with her over-sized burnt orange sweater.

She offers me a friendly wave. "Hi, there. Welcome to Turn the Page. What can I do for you?"

I swallow reflexively, my nerves getting the better of me, before I finally admit, "I'm looking for Kennedy. Kennedy Barnes. I heard she owns the place."

"Oh, Kennedy did. But she lets me run the place these days. My name is Shannon. Maybe there's something I could do for you instead."

As quickly as my stomach dropped to the floor to hear that Kennedy doesn't own the bookstore anymore, my chest fills with sudden hope when she tells me her name.

Maybe it's a coincidence. Just because the new owner of the shop happens to have the same name as one of the four listed inside of the grimoire... it could be a coincidence.

Please don't let it be a coincidence...

"You might be able to help. You see, I'd like to ask you about a book."

"Sure thing. Shoot. What's the title?"

"Um. It's called the *Grimoire du Sombra*."

Shannon's face freezes for a few seconds and I know then and there that this ain't no coincidence.

Thank God.

She recovers after a moment. "Sounds familiar. Do you have it with you?"

No. Because I'm a fucking idiot. I only realized when I was getting off of the Parkway that, in my mad dash to leave my house, I left it in my bedroom. I plopped it on my nightstand as I got everything I thought I might need in case this actually becomes a rescue mission, then completely blanked on grabbing it.

"I don't."

"Oh."

I'm losing her. She's going to act like she can't help me... unless I give her a reason to.

"I saw your name." At least, I *think* it's her name. "You and Kennedy. Some kid named Amy, too, and Susanna... her script looks like the same handwriting next to the 'true love' spell. Maybe it was her book first.

It's mine now. Well, Sammael's... but he's gone. They *took* him."

Shannon blinks.

Okay. So maybe I shouldn't have unloaded all of that on a stranger if I didn't want her thinking I was a lunatic, but I'm desperate.

And then she says, "Sammael? You know Sammael?"

Hang on—

"*You* know Sammael?"

Instead of answering my question, she comes waddling out from behind the counter. And, hell, I do mean *waddling*. From chin to chest, you never would've guessed what she was hiding beneath that sweater, but as Shannon scoots past me, heading for the door, I can't help but gape.

With the low belly on her, she's gotta be like eight or nine months pregnant.

Too busy staring, I don't realize what she's doing until I hear the lock on the front door *snick* shut, followed by her pressing down on the switches, killing all of the lights.

And, whoa, maybe I shouldn't even *think* the word 'killing' right now...

"Um. Is everything okay?"

"Huh?" Shannon must see the guarded look on my face because she laughs. "Sorry if I scared you. It's close enough to closing to shut down a little early, and

I think... yeah. This is a conversation we should take upstairs."

Upstairs? "I don't understand."

She points at the ceiling. "I have a small studio built above the store. It used to be Kennedy's apartment, but she gave it to me and I gave it to Mal. You should meet him."

"And he can't come down to the store?"

"No. He can't."

Oh. Never mind. I *do* understand.

"Ah. You got it." She grins, tucking a stray strand of her blonde hair behind her ear. "Come on. Follow me upstairs."

***

MAL, IT TURNS OUT, IS REALLY MALPHAS.

Another seven-foot-tall demon with black horns, red skin, but *golden* eyes, he is Shannon's bonded mate.

The studio she mentioned is his. An artist from Sombra, he lives with her in the human world, staying out of sight, and working on his paintings while she runs the store she took over when Kennedy decided to stay with her Sombra demon mate in the other world.

Because, yup. Kennedy has a mate, too, and I actually got to meet him. It's Loki, the demon who showed up with the soldier to take my mate.

I tell them everything. It's so much easier to just

word vomit, getting it all out instead of obsessing over what could be happening to Sammael right now. Shannon interrupts a few times to ask questions, while Mal just sets his paintbrush down and moves closer as though instinctively protecting his mate from the threat of another demon coming to take her.

At least I finally understand what was up with Loki having the name 'Kennedy' carved into his chest like that. One glimpse of Malphas and I see that he's wearing 'Shannon' on his.

It's a Sombra demon thing, kind of like wedding rings for humans.

I have a hundred questions to ask them. They're living proof that a human and a demon can have a successful relationship, and maybe after I find Sammael, I'll have to take another trip to Jericho with him to visit Shannon and her mate.

I just have to get to him, first.

When I finally finish my explanation, Shannon bobs her head. "Okay. So they took him to Sombra. Do you know where?"

"I don't know."

"You bonded yourself to him, right? Got some of that shadow dick? You have his essence. Use it."

Shannon might be one of the most entertaining women I've ever met. She obviously has no filter, but she's helping me so I'm just gonna look past the easy way she refers to mating Sammael as 'getting shadow dick'.

"How do I do that?"

"I... I can't really explain it," Shannon says. "You just... you do it. It's like tapping into them to find out what makes them tick. It's instinctive."

Before it gave me a headache, I could do that with Sammael. But since he's been gone...

I shake my head. "I can't."

"The chains," offers Malphas. "When Nox wore them, he said they cut him off from his Amy. Maybe it's the same for Sammael and his Hope."

Look at that. So grown-up Amy also has a mate. I bet Susanna does as well, and if I can find a way to get Sammael back, maybe I'll add my name to the book, too.

Then again, maybe not. Shannon is taking me showing up here like a crazy person a whole lot better than I would if I were in her shoes. That's the last thing I need. Some other demon's mate tracking me down at the library to ask me questions...

No, thanks.

I just want Sammael. That's all. I want my mate back, and to begin planning what forever after looks like with him.

I get my first glimpse watching Malphas and Shannon. From what she tells me, they've been together for more than a year, they have a home together, and a family they're getting ready to add on to.

They're happy.

I want that—but not if I can't get to Sammael.

"I don't even know why they put him in chains. He said that humans aren't allowed to know about him. They don't! It's just me. There's no reason to take him as a prisoner."

Shannon snorts. "There doesn't have to be a reason, Hope. Sending demons after the good guys, putting them in chains or threatening to… that's just what the demon dickhead does."

"My flower…"

Shannon rolls her eyes, lips quirked in a small grin. "Sorry, babe. I meant *demon duke.*"

"Duke Haures," rumbles her mate. "The ruler of Sombra."

"Big guy. Crazy white skin and creepy blue eyes." Shannon reaches up, waving over her ponytail. "He wears a crown, too, in case the throne and the castle and the guards everywhere in the capitol don't make it obvious he runs the show. Just another reason why me and Mal stick around Jericho unless we have to go to the healer to check up on our kiddo."

I know I shouldn't let it distract me. But now that she mentions it…

"I'm sorry." It's been bothering me from the moment I put two and two together and realized that she was about to pop—and that her Sombran mate is the father. "But humans and demons... so 'shadow dick' really leads to... I don't know... hybrid babies?"

"That's what they tell me. Since I'm the first we know who's gonna give birth, I guess we'll all find out." With an amused gleam in her eyes, she leans in and says, "We got a pool going on if my kiddo's gonna eventually come out with horns or not."

"We? I thought no one is supposed to know that Sombra demons exist."

That's what Sammael told me. He used magic to take Johanna's memories of him from her, and he tried to do the same to me before they dragged him away. Good thing it didn't work on me, but if he didn't have to do that to my sister...

"Oh, yeah. Big trouble if anyone finds out. Chains, remember? Woof." Shannon shakes her head, long blonde ponytail swaying with the motion. "Not fun. That's why, when I say 'we' like that, I mean the other mates. Amy thinks horns are a 'yes'. Kennedy's praying it's a 'no' because she can't imagine what they'll do to her vagina on the way out. Me, I was a toss-up until Kennedy said that and now I'm a 'hell fucking no' because yikes, right?"

"Fear not, my mate," rumbles Malphas. "I shall continue to love your cunt no matter what happens to it."

Shannon laughs, bumping up against his side. "You better, big guy. You're the one who did this to me."

Malphas drapes one arm over her shoulder before bowing over her, cradling her bump. "To bring more Shannon into this realm or any other... it is my greatest masterpiece."

Ugh. Normally, I would think it was adorable how much they obviously love each other. Now? It's sickeningly cute, mainly because I'm super fucking jealous.

Clearing my throat, drawing their attention back to me, I ask them with a desperate edge to my voice, "Can you help me find him?" Shannon just said she goes back to Sombra for the healer. I lift my eyes, meeting Malphas's hypnotic gold ones. "Can you make one of those portal things to bring me to Sombra?"

I just need to get to the other world. Once there, I can start searching for my demon, but it's pointless to even try if I'm stuck on the other side of some veil that shouldn't even exist.

"If my mate allows it," Malphas says solemnly.

"Hell, yeah," Shannon answers. "Who are we to stand in the way of true love, right? I mean, if it was Glaine, I might think twice, but Sammael seems alright to me. Come on." She nudges Malphas, then grins over at me. "What are we waiting for?"

The answer to that, it seems, is nothing.

Unlike me, who overthinks everything and has to

come up with a plan even when I'm acting impulsively, Shannon truly is impulsive. Once Malphas agrees to open a portal, she points at the space right in front of her and says, "Chop, chop, Mal. Portal us up, would you, babe?"

"As you wish," is his response before the big demon waves his red hand, forming a hole right where she wanted.

It's different. I don't see the flames that were visible in Loki's, only deep black shadows, but Malphas and Shannon both assure me that this will work.

I only just met them. I want to believe them... and I end up doing so, only going after Shannon hops in, big belly and all, before Malphas brings up the rear.

My first reaction is to think that they opened up a portal straight into an oven; if not that, this is truly Hell. I mean it. The air is so hot, it hurts to breathe at first, and everything seems to have a dusty tinge of red to it. The ground is soft, and when I look down to see why it's shifting beneath my weight, I notice that it's because it's freaking *ash*.

My mom smoked before she passed. I know what ash looks like.

The air smells like it, too. A mix of cigarette and rotten eggs, I cough, then groan when the heat nearly scorches my lungs.

Shannon pats me on the back. "Welcome to Sombra, Hope. Don't worry. You get used to it."

What a lovely thought.

As I get my coughing under control, I look around. It's darker here, dimmer than the human world, and I guess that's because it is a shadowy realm. Squinting, hoping my eyes don't dry out, I begin to see the various different buildings surrounding us.

It looks like Malphas's portal has dropped me off right in the middle of some village square.

"This is Nuit," he says, answering the question I didn't even get to ask yet. "This is my clan."

Is it Sammael's? The only thing I remember him mentioning is Mavro and the School of Mages which is just another reminder that I don't know him. Not really.

But I was supposed to get forever to learn him—and that's exactly what I plan on having.

And, just when I turn to get my bearings, trying to figure out what my next move is going to be, a high-pitched female voice calls out.

"Shannon! What are you doing here? I thought you weren't due to come back and see the healer for another cycle!"

I turn around, but Malphas is standing right in front of me. I can't see around him, though I do hear Shannon chuckle, then say, "Hey, Kennedy. I brought company."

"Company?"

I guess that's my cue.

I step out from behind Malphas's bulk. I see

another human woman, with a heart-shaped face, wavy brown hair, and a belly much smaller than Shannon's.

When she sees me, Kennedy gasps.

I wave. "Hi. I'm Hope."

Shannon jerks her thumb at me. "She's Sammael's mate."

Because I am, aren't I?

IT LOOKS LIKE I GOT TO MEET KENNEDY BARNES, AFTER all. Only, instead of finding her at Turn the Page, she lives in Sombra with a mate of her own—and, like Shannon, she's currently pregnant.

No wonder she's worried about the horns on her kid. I don't plan on shacking up with Sammael on the gold moon anytime soon if that's what I have to look forward to, but it looks like it's too late for her.

Of course, considering how devoted she is to her mate, she doesn't seem to mind...

I'm currently inside of her house. In her self-proclaimed living room, she has a couch made of shadows that looks like something you could get back home. When I mention that, she proudly tells me that her mate conjured it for her. The same thing for the two chairs that Shannon and me are currently sitting on, with Malphas standing with his hand on the back of his mate's seat.

Kennedy is sitting on Loki's lap, snuggling up against her demon mate. I get the idea it's one part because she's still in the honeymoon stage and doesn't want to be separated from him, and the other part because her... well, her pet is used to sitting on the other side of the couch.

I say 'pet'. That's what that thing is, according to Kennedy. Its fur is shadows, its eyes are a blinding white, and whenever I look at it right, I can see features that make it look like a little bit like a squirrel—that's the fluffy tail and pointed snout—and a cat—that's the pointed ears and the long, narrow body. Loki calls it an ungez, Kennedy calls it Freya, and I just hope it doesn't bite.

To be on the safe side, I avoid the critter.

I almost do the same to Kennedy's mate.

At first, I do. I want to hate Loki just on principle since he was the one who put the chains on Sammael, but when I learn that he only did it because he respected Sammael—his former mentor—and wanted to help him if he could, I begrudgingly stop giving him the stink-eye.

He didn't seem so surprised when Kennedy invited us into her house, either. Diplomatically ignoring the way I scowled when I first saw him, the demon actually snorts.

"Despite his insistence, I didn't really think Sammael could give up his mate so easily," he said in a deep, rumbling voice. "The gods know I would never let my Kennedy go."

Kennedy's reaction was to murmur something about how she figured that out when he kidnapped her and brought her to Sombra.

That definitely caught my attention for a moment, and I admit Loki and his human mate living together in Sombra is a story I'd love to hear another day. For now?

I just want to find a way to get Sammael.

It isn't long before I understand why Malphas's portal brought us to Nuit. If the demon duke has my mate—and Loki confirms that that was where the green-eyed demon soldier took him—then he would be in the capital city of Sombra, a shimmering blue oasis known as Mavro that is the epicenter of this hellish realm.

As a clan artist, Malphas can only summon a portal between the human world where his human mate summoned him to and the village where she summoned him from. That's where the hole in the veil between realms exists for him. In order to travel from Nuit to Mavro, I needed to be a Sombra demon myself who can travel vast distances in their shadow form—or I needed a demon mage who could conjure portals.

I needed Loki.

With Shannon's help, I explain to Kennedy and Loki who I am and why I'm here. Having been the one to give me enough of a clue that I found my way to Sombra in the first place, Loki is impressed by my ingenuity and how quickly I was able to cross over to the demon realm in search of my mate.

And yet... when I ask him—and maybe it was more like I *beg* him to bring me to the infamous Duke Haures so that I can plead my case—the double-horned demon hesitates.

"Sammael deserves his mate," he says after a moment. "And the gods know that this female is determined to claim him... but will you do so when facing Duke Haures? Because, if you do not, there might be a pair of chains in it for you."

That's the same thing that other demon tried to threaten me with. I'm not worried about that, though. I didn't break any rules, and since there's no denying that I'm Sammael's mate, he didn't, either. The first law says humans aren't allowed to know about Sombra. He fixed Jo so that she didn't, and then I bonded myself to him.

We should be in the clear, and I have no problem telling this Haures guy that.

Just like I have no problem telling Loki that, either.

I can tell he's on the edge. He has a sense of loyalty to Sammael since my mate used to be Loki's teacher centuries ago, but Duke Haures is the big guy in charge. Loki seems much happier staying with his pregnant mate in their tiny village as far from the capital as they can get...

Until Kennedy places her hand under his chin, guiding him to look at her.

"Will you help her, babe?" she murmurs just loud enough that I can hear her. "For me?"

He slides the edge of his thumb along the height of her cheek. "I will do anything for you, my heart."

And that is exactly how, the same day he chained up my mate and stole him away from me, I find myself hitching a ride to Mavro with the other demon mage.

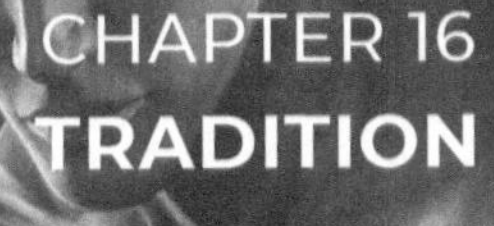

CHAPTER 16
TRADITION

SAMMAEL

Over the centuries, I've been in the dungeons beneath Duke Haures's castle countless times. Always acting as his mage, either conjuring the chains I now wear before removing them from the prisoners when the duke released them—or decided that they deserved the shadows rather than a cell.

I should be grateful that Duke Haures didn't command Glaine to bring me right to the edge of Sombra. When my comrade made it clear that it wasn't revealing myself to my mate that earned me the chains but stealing the grimoire and casting the matefinder spell that angered our leader, I'd expected to face his wrath immediately.

I have not yet, but it will come. Duke Haures suffers no fool, and anyone who is a danger to his mate is eliminated. I know that better than most. The first law is unbreakable, too. I spent many cycles in the human world; it was inevitable that Duke Haures would use me to make an example to the rest of Sombra.

Only... I thought, if I wasn't meant for the shadows, I'd at least have to explain myself to my lord. He had trusted me, believing that I would deliver the ancient book to the human world, then return to continue in my post as his personal mage. When I did not, I betrayed him.

I expected to be dragged in front of him instead of being tossed to the dungeons, though maybe I shouldn't have. The duke couldn't have made it any clearer that I was no use to him any longer than by abandoning me to a cell with Glaine the only one to visit me since, bringing me two meals.

He is quiet both times. The Glaine I know—the soldier I've worked alongside for centuries—is not usually so introspective. It's as though he has some-thing on his mind, the glow in his green eyes fading as he keeps our meetings short. All he wanted to know was if it was true, if I did bind Hope to me in the small amount of time that I wasn't a phantom. The truth wouldn't save me from the chains, but I couldn't lie to Glaine.

Not about that.

Not after I had already deceived him by letting him think that I used magic to erase myself from Hope's memories before I allowed my protege to clasp the chains on my wrists.

I am a selfish male. A selfless demon would have sacrificed their freedom for their mate—which I did, gladly—but he would also have taken the mark he left on his female with him. The chains won't break the bond I have with Hope, though they do dull the connection existing between us; between the chains and the veil between realms, I can't sense her at all. She's safe in the human world, and she would've been content, believing that the one night we shared was nothing but a pleasant dream if I'd made her think it was so.

But I... I could not. I would treasure the small amount of time I spent with my beloved for the rest of my existence, but just as I was about to cast the spell to make her forget me, I found myself unable to.

I wanted her to remember me. Returning to Sombra, accepting the penalty for what I did all those cycles ago... I could do that with my horns held high so long as, in another world, Sammael still existed for his Hope.

After all, she is all I exist for now.

WHEN I HEAR THE SOLID STEPS HEADING DOWN THE corridor leading toward my cell, I frown.

With the chains on, I can only access my solid demon form. As chilly as the dungeons are—so much cooler than even Duke Haures's garden oasis—I was able to conjure enough shadow coverings for the lower half of my body. Between that and the blankets Glaine brought for my bedding, I'm as comfortable as I can expect to be even though I have not been able to rest just yet.

I don't know how long it's been since I left Hope behind. Too long, and I know I'll see her when I dream... but it won't be the same as when I actually *saw* her on the dream plane.

But all of that explains why I'm trapped in my demon shape. In the dungeons, all of the palace guards drift around in the shadow form in case they need to move much quicker than they can on their feet since only mages can create portals to travel through.

So why do I hear footsteps?

A moment later, when a large frame appears in front of my cell, flanked by two shadow demons—one with green eyes, the other gold—I know the answer to my question.

I've worked directly for Duke Haures since I graduated from the School of Mages. Aside from Susanna and possibly Dagon, I can say that I know the ruler of Sombra the best of any other of his subjects. And yet...

I've never seen him appear in any shape other than his demon form.

Rumors have spread for centuries that he only has the one shape. That it was the mark of the demon destined to lead, the same as his eerily white skin. No other Sombrans are as pale as he, all of us with skin as red as the ash fields during the morning sun. And his eyes... I've never seen anyone with blue eyes the same color as Mavro's oasis apart from Duke Haures himself.

I bow my head, awarding the ruler of Sombra my respect. To see that he's come to visit me in the dungeons... I don't know his motives, but I cannot imagine they are to my benefit.

The green-eyed demon is Harth, another one of Duke Haures's personal guard. I know the golden-eyed demon as well. A craftsman from the village just outside of Mavro, he is Candor, the local male who specializes in marking newly bonded demons with the name of their females.

What is he doing here? Harth, I understand. Duke Haures, yes. But Candor?

When the duke clears his throat, his signal that I've shown him enough respect that I can now dare look him in the eye, I stand straight again.

Harth has drifted away, standing near the break in the corridor. Candor, a shadow-woven bag hanging loosely from his claws, is standing right behind the duke.

Duke Haures is watching me unblinkingly, his expression flat. "Sammael."

I nod. "My lord."

"It pains me to see you on the other side of these bars, but you left me no choice."

I know. "She was my mate," is all I can say. For a bonded male like Duke Haures, that should be enough for him to understand—but he isn't just a bonded male. He's responsible for every soul in Sombra, and that means that he must do what's best for all of us.

He believes that fraternizing with the humans is a danger to all demonkind. I must admit... as much as I love my Hope with every fiber of my being, I learned enough of the human world to know that he is right. There is a reason why Sombra and Earth cannot coexist. There is a reason why keeping the mortal and immortal worlds separate serves as Duke Haures's first law.

I didn't break it. Only one human who was not my mate learned of my existence, but I did erase the memory of my summoning from Hope's female kin. Her sister. I kept to the tenets in the law—but that's not why I'm here in this cell, wearing a prisoner's chains.

And I am, all because...

"About the book—"

Duke Haures cuts me off with a wave of his hand. He has no magic, not like a mage, but I go silent at the gesture regardless. "Is it still in the human realm?"

Hope has it. "Yes."

"Then I care nothing about the *Grimoire du Sombra*. You did what I expected you to. You brought the book to the human realm where it belongs and that's where it'll stay." Duke Haures's eyes cut through the shadows in the dungeons. "I also expected your return to Sombra long before I had to send my favored soldier after you."

"I am sorry—"

He silences me again with another glance. "For what? For doing what a male in need of his mate is fated to do?"

I blink. That almost sounds as though I'm forgiven... "Your grace?"

"I know everything about my subjects. Especially those I keep close. I know *you*, Sammael. From the moment you left with the book, I expected this as well. But I also know that us Sombra demons aren't meant to wield those spells on our own without... complications."

Complications... yes. You can say that is what happened to me after I cast the spell and it turned me into a phantom until I found a way to convince Hope to read the manifestation herself.

"Four cycles," he continues. "In the human realm, at least. Here, we've seen the gold moon pass twice— but you only just mated your female. You only just gave her your essence. Do you know why that is?"

Duke Haures never asks a question that he doesn't already know the answer to himself. Just like he would've known that I found my mate but could not reach her, he had to have suspected that the spell failed on me, leaving me as a phantom.

His expression does not change at all as I tell him everything. Only then, when I finish my tale by admitting that I finally found a way to reach Hope, first through my dreams, then through her wee-jee board summoning, does he nod.

"That's exactly what I thought. Of course, I couldn't go to the human realm myself to prove my suspicions right. I had to bring you here. And since you *did* defy me... I see no reason why I can't keep you here while I wait to meet your mate."

My mate? Hope?

"That won't be possible, your grace."

Duke Haures has a surprisingly lovely laugh. I've always thought so, and he shows it off now. "And why is that, Sammael? Because you used magic to make her forget you?"

I don't answer. He would know if I lied, and I don't want to admit the truth.

I don't have to.

"You bonded your mortal to you. Glaine confirmed it, and my guard is still loyal. And yet... while he insists you said you would, I know better. She remembers you, and if she's truly meant to be your gods-given mate, she will find her way to you sooner or later." His blue eyes glimmer. "Even with the chains."

I know exactly what he's referring to. Nox met his human mate when she was spawn, imprinting on her though he could not bond her to him since she was not yet a mature female. For fourteen human years, he stayed in a cell just like this one, wearing the same chains... but despite being on different planes, his mate reached through the veil, calling him to her.

Nox found a way to momentarily slip free from his chains so that he could answer her call. Apart from mages, only Sombra demons who have been summoned to different realms can return to them— and the hunter did.

He loved her too much to ignore her call. If Hope needed me, I would go to her, too.

But will my human call? We're bonded, our instincts taking over shortly after the summoning, but though I love her, does she feel the same?

I had wanted more time. To show her that I can be the best male for her, her one true mate... and I got one moon before I had to say goodbye.

It was worth it. I won't deny that. It was worth it— and from the way I look through the bars, meeting Duke Haures head-on, I show him that, given the opportunity, I would do the same thing all over again.

Duke Haures meets my stare, then surprises me by gesturing for Candor. Then, as the craftsman moves next to him, he grabs the bar nearest to him, curving his claws around it. "In here," he says.

As a shadow, Candor contracts until he's thin enough to pass through the bars, joining me in my cell.

Before I can question it, Duke Haures says, "There's a reason why us demons mark ourselves with the names of our mates."

I nod. "It is tradition."

A Sombra male is proud to show off the female—demoness or human—who he gave his essence to.

"Yes, there is that. But it's also so the male can show who he belongs to. Who blessed him with their essence, claiming him in return. It's our promise that we'll protect our females. And you, Sammael... you're a bonded male with a bare chest."

Of course. Because I only just bonded Hope to me—but, to Duke Haures, that is no excuse.

And that's how I know that, while I might be in the dungeons for now, it's only until the duke decides to let me return to my mate.

Whenever that will be...

HOPE

Mavro is the capital city of Sombra. I don't get to see it for myself, but I know enough about it from Sammael that it's an oasis in the center of their hellish realm. When I try to dig deeper, rifling through his memories, all I get is a single name: *Haures.*

It's the same name that I heard from Malphas in Jericho, then from Loki when he agreed to bring me to meet with the infamous demon duke. He's the ruler of the entire demon world, the powerful guy that Sammael served under before he came to find me in my world, and the only person I can appeal to to get me my mate back.

After all, Sammael is only in Sombra on the duke's

orders, and that means he's the only one who can release him.

As the duke's replacement mage, Loki is allowed to use one of his portals to take him right into the throne room where the ruler of Sombra meets with his subjects. Other demons are able to use shadow travel —which is just what it sounds like, turning into the faintest form of their shadow and passing through the circles cut into the roof, almost like they're flying— while Loki's way of crossing from Nuit to the capital is way faster.

I'm still not used to how the portals work. The one that brought me from Jericho to Sombra in the first place was full of flames that didn't burn me. Loki's portals are pitch-black, made up of shadows, and they leave me stumbling when I move through them.

Luckily, he's there to grip my arm and steady me so that I don't fall flat on my face in front of the impressive duke of Sombra.

Because, whoa, is everything about him and his glimmering palace *impressive*.

At the far end of the room, raised up on a dais about three feet off the smooth floor I'm standing on, is a crystalline throne that would make Shaq look like he's sitting in his daddy's chair. It's freaking *huge* which makes sense when I see the massive male sitting on it.

Shannon's flippant description of Duke Haures nailed him to a tee. Unlike every other demon I've seen, his solid form is straight-up white, though the blue moon shining through the gaps in the ceiling paint him a softer version of the color. He has long, thick white hair, shocking blue eyes, a crown perched on his head, and fangs that grow upward like tusks.

He's wearing something similar to chainmail that, honestly, does nothing to hide those honking, huge muscles of his. When he speaks, I almost expect him to grunt, and I'm shocked when his voice comes out smooth and surprisingly gentle.

"Loki," he calls, addressing the demon who brought me here. "What is this?"

Oh, shit. Because Shannon knew about the duke, and so did Loki's mate, I figured the demon duke was all aboard the "humans bonding with demonkind" train. But the way he just said that... does he even know what a human is?

"This is Hope," Loki says, gesturing at me with his shadowy hand.

"She's a human female. A mortal."

Scratch that. He definitely knows what I am. Somehow, that doesn't make me feel any better than I did before.

Loki nods. "She is also Sammael's mate."

Duke Haures steeples his claws, lounging back on his elaborate throne. "Ah. Is she now?" His lips curve, appearing like a sneer around his fangs, though I don't think he means to look so ferocious. "I was wondering if she would find her way to Sombra. Since I've been told that she was supposed to have no memories of this place, I doubted she would... and, yet, here she stands."

And thank God for that. I don't know if it's because I'm his bonded mate and it wouldn't have worked, or if Sammael refused at the last minute because he wanted me to remember him, but it doesn't matter. What's done is done, now I'm here, and I need to figure out how I'm going to find a way to get the fearsome demon duke to let Sammael go.

I'm not the type of woman who knows how to wheedle, or how to dance around the subject so that I can manipulate someone else into doing what I want them to. This is like Jake all over again. Before I knew that I was meant for a shadow demon, anyone with a dick was looking good to me. I still wanted to sleep with someone I knew, someone I was attracted to, and someone that was interested in me, too, but I didn't coyly try to get Jake to ask me out again, hoping the night would end with us in bed.

Oh, no. I asked *him* to dinner, then invited him back to my house, making it pretty fucking clear that— if it wasn't for my stomach turning against me—I would've invited him up to my bedroom next.

So, staring up at the intimidating duke, I'm not trying to come up with a plan. I wish I could, but the only thing I do is blurt out, "I'm here to bring Sammael back. He's supposed to be my mate and I want him."

It's the truth. No matter what, if I was impulsive and reckless or if this is the first 'right' thing I've done in my adult life, I don't care... I kinda understood what I was getting into when I mated him. When I bonded myself to him. The promise was a little sketchy since I didn't understand Sombran yet, but I think of that as my demon wedding.

I made my vows. For good or for bad, I'm going to stand by them.

It's all because of the acorns, I think with sudden clarity as the demon duke looks down at me without saying a damn word. For weeks, Sammael left acorns in front of my door, trying to show me affection while I had no idea he was even there.

That's not all he did, either. He put my keys on their ring, using more energy than he should to take care of me. He made sure my slippers were always together. Little things that he could pull off while he was still a ghost, he did it all for me because—even before I knew he was real, he thought of me as his.

Now it's my turn to treat him like he's *mine*.

Finally, Duke Haures asks, "How far are you willing to go to earn his freedom?"

"Freedom?" *Freedom*? "Hang on... where is Sammael? Where did you put him?"

"In my dungeons."

What?

"He's my prisoner. He stole from me." Then, as

though he wants to really rub the salt in my sudden wound there, he adds, "He stole the book that called you to him."

So?

"Yeah? I'm sorry, but I don't really care how I found out we were meant for each other. But if you, like, arrested him because of the book, I can go back home and get it. Take it. Just let me have Sammael back."

"You'd do that?"

I nod decisively. "Yes."

His eyes light up. "And I'll ask you again, female: what will do you to earn his freedom?"

Impulsive, frantic Hope strikes again as I promise the duke, "*Anything.*"

"Very well. Then I would have you enter the shadows at the end of Sombra and bring me back an ashbalm flower."

Behind me, Loki lets out a rush of air. A sigh almost, or maybe a sound of resignation. I'm not sure, but before I can ask why the duke seems so triumphant and the other mage so defeated, a soft, lilting voice carries through the throne room.

"Haures, my love. What is going on here?"

There is a door along the wall to my left that I didn't notice before. It's open now, revealing a garden and a pond, everything tinged with blue, almost sparkling from this distance.

Silhouetted against the lovely backdrop are two

figures. One of them is a shadow demon all in black with a pair of fierce red eyes peering into the throne room. He has horns that twist on the end before jutting straight up toward the ceiling, though the rest are his features are more nondescript since he's far enough away that the shadows hide them.

Standing a good head shorter than the demon is another human woman. She has long, wavy dark hair with skin that seems so much tanner compared to Duke Haures's pure white color. Her dress flows like silk; it matches the demon duke's blue eyes exactly. She's slender, yet tall, with an almost ageless beauty.

The brunette looks at me, a shocked expression twisting her pretty face. "Who is this? And why are you asking her to retrieve ashbalm for you?"

I thought I was being reckless, daringly mouthing off to the duke. This woman addresses him pretty boldly, not even using his title or anything.

"Dagon," Duke Haures says, purposely not answering her question, "please bring my mate back to her quarters."

Ah, well. That'll do it.

Huh. Did Sammael know that the duke had a human mate of his own? I wouldn't have been so damn scared of him if I knew that myself, but I guess this is another one of those 'don't ask, don't know' situations where I can't find the answer in his download if I don't know to ask the question in the first place.

I get the idea that the duke doesn't like anyone to know about his human mate. Not because he's ashamed or embarrassed or anything, but because he prefers to keep her tucked away, out of sight and protected.

But now that she's seen me, I think that's off the table for the moment.

"I would really like to stay."

"Su..."

"My love. Please."

The duke doesn't argue again. With a brisk nod, he says, "Very well. Dagon, stay close to her while I finish this."

The human woman—*Su*—crosses toward the dais, stepping up to it so that she's standing beside the throne. She looks so tiny next to the duke, but I know from experience that size only matters where it counts with these demon guys. At the very least, if I take the lovey-dovey look on her face as she peers up at the duke as any clue, she's not being held here against her will.

The other demon—who must be Dagon—drifts within arm's reach of the brunette, always staying at her back.

He also stays quiet.

Su doesn't. "What is this all about?" she asks again. "I thought I heard you mention the ashbalm."

"You did."

She frowns. "You're not going to let this girl find some, are you?"

This girl? I've only got two years until I'm thirty, and maybe I have a young-ish face, but I'm definitely not a girl.

Then again, when you take into account that any human who bonds with a Sombra demon gets to live forever with their new mate out of the deal, she could be just as old as Sammael is... and then I really would be a girl in comparison.

Duke Haures lays his hand on the arm of his throne, palm up. Su immediately places hers against his.

"It must be done. You did it."

"I know. It's just... never mind. I shouldn't have interfered."

"No. You must always know that I treasure your input. But in this... I couldn't do it for you, my mortal. I cannot do it for Sammael's, either."

She nods, clinging to his fingers. "You're right. And getting the ashbalm flower was the least of what I had to do to become your mate. But I would do it all again in a heartbeat to be yours."

There's that lovey-dovey look again. And to think I started questioning my own sanity when I decided to go all in with a shadow demon I had barely met just because he was ready to commit from the jump... this other human woman looks like the freaking sun rises and sets with the duke.

I guess there really is someone out there for everyone.

Her piece said, Su closes her eyes—so strangely dim now that I've gotten used to looking at Sombrans—and murmurs just loud enough for it to travel, "I think I'd like to return to the garden for now. Haures, my love... I'll be waiting for you there for when this business is done."

"Soon," the demon duke promises.

Su nods her head absently before dropping her lips down to press a kiss to his meaty palm. Then, without another look at anyone else, she slips around the back of his throne, gliding toward the open door that leads outside.

Halfway there, Duke Haures points his inch-long claw after her. "Dagon," he rumbles.

It's not necessary. As though he's the brunette's shadow, the red-eyed demon had already followed behind her.

Okay, then.

The duke waits until his mate and her guard have disappeared, the door sliding behind them, before he seems to remember what was going on before his mate found her way to the throne room. He probably wishes he could just get up and follow her himself, but at the last moment, he pulls himself together, once again the powerful ruler of the demon realm.

"My request is very simple. You want your mate. I want you to bring me an ashbalm flower. Do that, and I'll bring Sammael out of the dungeons for you."

Sounds good. "Where do I get one?"

"They're found along the inner edges of the shadows at the end of Sombra. Loki will bring you there, and he'll wait for you to best the shadows—or to fail them."

Fail them... oh, I don't like the way he said that.

But what else can I do?

"Fine," I say, exhaling roughly. "You've got a deal."

"Yes," murmured the duke. "I thought I might."

HOPE

t turns out that the edge of the shadows where I'm supposed to find this one specific flower for the demon duke is located just past Nuit.

Loki points that out as he leads me through another portal, though I didn't need to see the structures in the distance behind us to recognize it. The stifling air weighing me down, the heat causing sweat to spring up along my brow... even the rotten egg stink is a pretty big clue that we're not in Mavro anymore.

My shoes sink into the fields of ash. At this point, I'm beginning to feel like a freaking ping pong ball, the way they have me going from the small village to the capital and back, and I'm ready to just get this over with so I can trade the flower for Sammael's freedom.

And just about then is when I notice the skulls popping out from the ash.

Like the village that Malphas and Shannon brought me to before, the ground is red covered with ash in varying shades of blacks, whites, and dingy greys. The sun—or maybe it's the moon, I can't really tell—is red, the rest of the sky a gloomy shade of dark grey a little bit softer than the ash.

I didn't notice the skulls right away. Bleached white, covered in the ash, it's only when I see one—complete with a twisted set of horns attached to the sides—only a few feet in front of me that I can't deny where Loki's brought me.

In a world full of immortal demons, I'm looking at the place they all go to die.

Duke Haures didn't tell me that. When I murmur my suspicions to Loki, all the other demon says is that he survived a hundred years in the shadows before he found his mate. It doesn't matter, though. As if Sammael is warning me from back at the duke's castle, he knows the true purpose of the shadows at the end of Sombra—and the monsters that call it home.

And I'm supposed to go in there.

The wall of impenetrable black shadows in front of me still manages to look alive which is daunting, considering I know this place signifies death for so many others. If I go too far off the main path, leaving the edges where the ashbalm flowers grow, I'd be little more than a snack for some of the beasts who hunt in the shadows.

The demons are hunters, too. This is where some of the villagers come to hunt for the meat that feeds them all. That's why I should be perfectly safe staying to the edges. The prey animals have learned to avoid it unless they want to end up on a plate, and those that are too stupid or weak to avoid being hunted shouldn't present a danger to me.

Shouldn't... but you never know, do you?

I could turn around and change my mind. Loki can make portals and it's not like he doesn't know how to open one into my house; he already did before so he could snatch my mate for the demon duke. Maybe Malphas and Shannon are still in Nuit and I can hitch a ride back to the human world with them.

Of course, I'd have to accept that Sammael is gone for good if I did that...

Breathe in, Hope. Hold it. Exhale.

Again.

Clenching my hands into fists at my side, I do my breathing exercises, trying to push back against my anxiety before I give in to it.

This is it.

Do I want to save Sammael?

I— yes. I do.

And that means I'm going in there for Duke Haures's flower. With nothing but my bare hands, the phone in my back pocket, and the irrational hope that the ruler of this world can be trusted, I'm going to do this.

I have no other choice.

I turn to Loki. Though I'm sure he'd much rather abandon me by the shadows and return to his pretty mate and that weird shadow cat-thing, he stays on the outside of the darkness, waiting for me to make up my mind.

I nod, psyching myself up. "Okay. I'm going to go get the flower now." Then, because you think it would've hit me before this moment, but it didn't because I'm letting my impulsive side take over, I ask, "Um... do you have any idea how I'm supposed to find it? Or what it looks like?"

The shadows are black. Odds are I'll be walking around blind once I pass through them. It's bad enough I'm looking for a flower I've never seen before, but what if I can't see at all?

Loki has an answer for that.

"Follow your nose." Using the tip of his claw, Loki taps his. "You'll know where to find the ashbalm flower when it calls to you."

Right. Because that helps. "And you're sure you can't come in with me?"

"Duke Haures insists that you go alone," he rumbles.

Yeah. I figured. "But you'll be here when I'm done? So I can bring him the flower and get my mate back?"

Loki lifts his hand, patting his inky black pec with the flat of his hand. It's so weird. As a walking, talking shadow creature, you'd expect his hand to either pass right through or, I don't know, meld into the mass of shadows that is Loki right now. It doesn't. He raps it, the sound echoing before being swallowed up by the impenetrable darkness ahead of me, then says in a solemn tone, "I vow it."

Instead of hovering off of the ground, his bare feet dig into the piles of ash that cover the reddish ground as though to prove he means it.

That's the best I'm going to get.

Okay. I suck in a breath, choking when Sombra's heat all but scorches my lungs. I wave him off when he leans toward me, though the mated demon is careful not to touch me. I have to remember that Sombra is nothing like New Jersey in October. The lingering stink of rotten eggs might not be too far off from some of the aromas you catch driving down the Turnpike, but even in the dog days of summer, the Jersey shore ain't nothing like this.

I want to go home. But since I want to go home with my new mate, I can't do that if I don't walk into the dark shadows first.

Good thing I brought my phone. I obviously don't

get service here, but so long as my flashlight app works, I'm not too worried about the shadows.

Oh, no. It's just what might be lurking in there that has me feeling like I'm going to piss myself...

Buck up, Hope. Get in, get the flower, get out. No biggie.

You can do this.

Unless you want to leave Sammael in the demon duke's dungeons, you have no choice.

Guilt's a big kick in the ass for me. So is my loyalty. If you're one of my people—whether that's my closest friends, my sister, my niblings—and you need me, that's one of the only times I can force myself out of my comfort zone.

Sammael is my mate, right? And I'm his. The only one he'll ever have, and the one he's waited centuries —*centuries!*—for. I might have only just met him, but he's my people now.

With a decisive jab of my thumb, I turn on my flashlight. Then, giving Loki a smile that's admittedly wavering a bit, I tell him, "I'll be right back."

And I only hope that I'm not full of shit.

I MAKE IT ABOUT TEN STEPS INTO THE SHADOWS BEFORE I lose my nerve and turn the brightness on my flashlight down to about twenty percent.

It's not as dark as I thought it would be. It's cooler, too; I swear, the temp's gone down about thirty degrees between one step and the next, cooling me off as soon as the shadows swallowed me whole. The moon overhead went from having a reddish hue to being a foreboding dark color that still somehow glows in the pitch-black of the sky.

There are no stars here, just that full, round moon and a sliver of the gold moon I've heard that belongs only in Sombra. And, yet, if I squint, I might actually be able to see without my flashlight.

But that's the thing. I don't *want* to. I already saw enough within those first few steps before I dimmed the light.

Inside of the shadows, appearing almost immediately, I can't avoid the piercing white eyes that are looking at me from all directions, starting with the ground up. Since all of the creatures that lurk here are made of shadows first and foremost, I can just about make out their shapes—and that's more than enough for me.

I swear, I even saw one that was big and bulky, almost like the black bear from the Turtleback Zoo, and when it got caught in my flashlight, it snarled so loudly that I whimpered and had to stop myself from fleeing.

Luckily, the faint stream of my flashlight keeps them all away from me; if I'm scared of them, they're definitely apprehensive when it comes to my phone. I hear some scurrying, some thudding, but with the light on full blast before, I got a much better idea of how *wrong* these shadow monsters are. Plus, there are bones. So many freaking bones inside the shadows. I thought the skulls lined up on the outskirts of the shadows were bad, but it looks like the predators just booted the skulls out into the ash. The rest of their poor victims are scattered around in here.

That's another reason why I have to lower the dimmer on my app. Sorry, but it's one thing to accept that this is a demon realm and that there are obviously dried bones in the ash. It's another to see them everywhere. The first few feet, I couldn't avoid them, though they're more spread out the further I go. Still, it's bad enough I have to hear them crunch under my shoe. I'd rather not see them at the same time.

Find the flower, Hope. Forget about the monsters and the bones and that, if I get turned around in here, I'm fucked. Duke Haures promised me that it was possible to get in, get the flower, and get out since the ashbalm grows closer to the edge of shadows. I shouldn't have to go *too* far, but if I do manage to get lost, I'm pretty sure they won't leave me in here to add to the piles of bones.

Besides, there's a good chance, if I give up and scream bloody murder, Loki would come and find me. He promised Kennedy that he'd help me, and that's after he already did, giving me the hint that started me on this path. If her demon is anything like mine, he will if I actually need him to—for her sake, and for mine because I'm Sammael's mate.

That thought in mind, I focus on what he told me to do just now: I follow my nose.

The stink of sulfur and rotten eggs is a lot fainter in the shadows so I'm not so sure what he wants me to do; it's still pretty powerful, and I hate to think how many shampoos it's going to take to get the odor out of my hair. I tiptoe a little further out, not wanting to go too far since the duke said *edges*, and gasp when a strange cookie-like scent suddenly forces its way through the acrid stench before slamming right into me.

Seriously.

Whatever it is, it's good enough to make my mouth water, but I pause when the scent triggers a memory that has my throat tightening in a good way.

It takes me a second to place the familiar smell and why it means so much to me, but I swear to God, it smells like the chocolate chip cookies my mom used to make every Christmas. I haven't smelled that aroma in years—mainly because not even Jo or I could cook them just right—but it touches me deep inside of my chest.

Huh. Is that what Loki meant? When he said that it would call to me? Because, not gonna lie, as soon as I catch a whiff of that, I actually want to go searching for the source of it. I know it won't be my mom—not with her gone these last six years now—but the familiar smell fills me with such a sense of nostalgia, love, and, yes, *hope* that I head right in the direction it's blowing in before I realize I've moved.

The delicious cookie smell grows stronger. I keep going, using my phone to guide my way, and when I see a hint of orange peeking through the shadows, my heart starts pounding against my ribcage.

The bones under my feet seem to crunch even louder, though the thud of my racing pulse nearly drowns out the sound as I hurriedly jog forward. Dropping my phone, covering the light with the back of my hand, hiding the screen against my hip, the orange glow blossoms into a small fire amongst the darkness.

And that's exactly what it turns out to be when I'm close enough to make out details. It's a black flower whose bloom is a constant, flickering flame set on top of its shadowy stem.

There's only one of these flowers growing from the ash. Hoping this is the *right* one, I drop low to the ground, careful to avoid the flame as I pluck the stem right out of the sandy dirt.

As soon as I do, the fire disappears. It doesn't even smolder; it's just gone. Not only that, but the stem beneath my gentle grip crumbles away. I wasn't expecting it, and I mutter a quick curse as I catch the tumbling flower in the hand holding my phone.

My screen illuminates the flower.

Shit.

The whole damn thing is made of ash, held together by a wish and a prayer. I probably should've been expecting that—I mean, the clue's right there in its name—and I just about stop breathing in case my exhale has it disintegrating.

After a few tense seconds, I admit that the flower is a little sturdier than that. Sure, part of the blossom fell away when it hit my phone, and half the stem is gone, but the rest of it is still intact.

Let's just hope I can keep it that way.

ASHBALM FLOWER

HOPE

I have never, ever felt so relieved in my life as when I take that last step out of the shadows.

The heat slams into me, but I was prepared. Besides, after the way I took tiny steps, going so slow that it seemed like an eternity passed between me plucking the flower and emerging back into the red sky and high temps of Sombra, I needed a little warmth to knock out the chill that had settled in my bones.

According to my phone—still clutched between white-knuckled fingers, hoisting up the ashbalm flower—I was in there for twenty-two minutes. At least fifteen of them were spent bringing the flower back.

But I did, and Loki is waiting outside for me just like he promised he would.

Still in his shadow form, he glides over to me. Without a word, he reaches for the flower.

I wasn't expecting *that,* either. I can't stop the big demon, and too stunned to really react, all I can do is say, "What? No—"

In my mind's eye, Loki grabs the ashbalm flower and it crumbles to dust in his massive hand. I'm already thinking about how I'll have to go back in there and see if I can find another flower and, oh my God, I really, really don't want to do that again and—

Oh.

Hang on.

Loki is gripping the stem between his claws, eyeing it closely with an expression that makes him appear as relieved as I was.

"Sammael said you were a resourceful human," marvels Loki, twirling the stem between his claws. Watching closely, my heartbeat slowing again, I notice that his claws actually pierce the wisps of the stem that are more shadows than ash.

Huh. I guess it's a Sombra thing. The demons can use their claws to hold the ashbalm flower while my human fingers are just too clumsy and make it fall apart almost instantly.

Swallowing my nerves, I cover up my earlier worry with a strained chuckle. "You know, you should do me a favor and carry that."

He immediately offers it back to me. "I cannot," he

says regretfully. "You must bring it to Duke Haures yourself."

Why am I not surprised? Bending my elbow, I jerk my chin at the crook. "Fine. But lay it there, please."

He does, and once he has, he asks, "Are you ready to return to Mavro?"

More than ready. "Yes."

His purple eyes lighten, closer to a soft lavender shade, as he moves his hand in front of him in a circular gesture. When he's done, a black oval hovers over the ground. He flexes his fingers, showing off his claws, then flings out his hand.

The oval moves with the gesture, growing, growing, growing until he's made another portal.

Loki goes first. Cradling the delicate ashbalm flower in my arm so that it doesn't crumble any further, I stumble into the portal, following after him.

Seconds later, the portal spits us out in the same blue-tinted room with the partially open roof I was in earlier.

Duke Haures is still lounging on his throne, looking ahead as though he'd spent the last half-hour or so waiting for our return. And maybe he did, maybe he had more faith in myself than me since he has a very familiar purple-eyed monster standing just in front of the dais that holds the duke's massive crystalline chair.

Sammael.

He's wearing the same golden chains I watched Loki conjure and clasp on my mate's thick wrists. His hands are folded at his waist, black shadows woven over his bottom half while the rest of him is the same solid, dark red shade he is when he's his solid demon form. The chains pool on the chilled floor, even cooler through the soles of my shoes after my trek through the ash fields, then the shadows.

"Hope." He breathes out my name. "You really are here in Sombra."

Did he doubt I would chase after him? Or did he think that, when the duke or one of his soldiers mentioned to him that I came all this way to claim him as mine, even going so far as to brave the shadows for that stupid flower, it couldn't be true?

That they were fucking with him?

It's strange, just how easy I can read his face. No... he didn't doubt me. But if he knows all about what kind of person Hope McReary is—from watching over me, plus the way he got a peek into my soul even before I agreed to bond myself to him—then he probably never expected I'd push past my anxieties and my fears to do everything I've done since he left me.

To be honest, if you'd asked me last week, I wouldn't have thought myself capable of it, either.

I guess I surprised the shit out of both of us.

I give him a crooked grin, drinking him in. When

he willingly walked through that fiery portal, I never thought I'd see him again, but he's here and he...

He...

Okay. He looks *different*.

It takes me a second to pinpoint what it is. Maybe I got used to the marks on Loki's chest, and on Malphas's, too, but even though I only spent a few nights with Sammael, I remember his beautifully sculpted chest intimately. His nipples were pretty and brown, standing out against his dark red skin, and there wasn't a bit of hair on him anywhere except for his head so it was smooth and hard and *delicious*.

It still is, only now? Sammael has four letters seemingly tattooed on his chest. They're silver and they shimmer, kind of like a mirror, and from this distance, I make out four letters: **S-P-E-S**.

For a heartbeat, I have no idea what that means, and my initial instinct is to think the worst. Both Loki and Malphas wear their human mate's names on their chests so of course I can't help but think that Sammael picked another girl after he came back to Sombra.

But then, as though it popped into my brain on its own—and, granted, it probably *did*—I suddenly understand that the word 'spes' is the concept of 'hope' in Sombran. It refers to the emotion of wanting something, needing something, expecting something to happen... and when he thinks of that, he thinks of me.

He left me behind to save me. He didn't erase my

memories like he did to Johanna, and even though he probably figured that we would never see each other again, he left me with a part of him—and then tattooed a memento of me on his chest.

I almost bolt for Sammael. He was right when he told me that the mate sickness would go away completely once we were bonded so it's not a need to rub myself all over him like a cat in heat that has me drawn to my mate. It's knowing that that's exactly what he is... that we're fated for each other... that has me eager to hold him, to hug him, to touch him again and prove that he's real.

Two things stop me.

First?

I went through hell—*literally*—to get this flower for Duke Haures. If I smoosh it because I hugged Sammael and the flower got caught between us, I'll never forgive myself.

And the second?

The glowering shadowy figure with the narrowed green eyes who has his wispy black claws digging into Sammael's shoulder warns me with just a glance against coming any closer to my mate.

I remember him. Green eyes. I didn't get that good of a look at him when it was Loki who had most of my attention in my bedroom, but those green eyes... I haven't forgotten them.

He's the soldier that ordered Loki to put Sammael

in chains. Glaine, I think he's called. Me, personally, I'd prefer 'Asshole', but I'm pretty sure his name was Glaine—and he's still standing guard over Sammael.

Everything from his stance to his expression makes it obvious. If I try to go near Sammael, he'll stop me.

So I don't. For now, I stay where I am, protecting the flower in my arms.

The last thing I need is to have made it this far only for the ashbalm flower to become a casualty now.

As though Duke Haures knows exactly what I'm thinking—and, honestly, he *might*—he clicks his claws together. "Good. You've returned, and so quickly, too. Now bring me the ashbalm."

Gladly.

Out of the corner of my eye, I notice that Sammael is watching me unblinkingly as I tiptoe my way across the floor. Again, I'm holding my breath, and I force myself to keep my gaze forward so that I don't trip or something at the last moment.

As soon as the duke uses his claws to snag the flower, I allow myself to exhale before I scurry back to where I was standing by Loki.

There. I have no idea why he needed me to get it, but I did—and now I want Sammael freed.

Again, Duke Haures proves that he must be some kind of mindreader because he tilts the ashbalm flower in my direction before I can ask about Sammael's chains. "Do you know why I had you retrieve this?"

No. I don't. Know why? Because the duke didn't tell me. All he said was that, if I wanted to see Sammael again, I had to bring him this stupid flower. I did it, Sammael is right there, and I'm ready for the two of us to go home and pretend none of this happened.

Hey. If Shannon and Malphas can make it work, living in the human world without anyone finding out about him, why can't me and Sammael? I have a house of my own without any roommates, and if Johanna comes by unannounced and sees him, I already know he can just *poof* his existence out of her brain.

Too bad it doesn't seem like a quick escape is likely. Not unless Duke Haures is willing to release Sammael and send us on our merry way...

He's watching me, waiting for my answer. Since I can't do anything else, I shake my head.

The duke searches out Sammael. "What of you, my mage? What do you know of the ashbalm flower?"

Sammael gulps. "Only that it blooms for those in need of it. I learned of it at the School of Mages. It's the only substance in all of Sombra that can interfere with a mate bond."

It *what*?

I didn't know that. How could I? When Duke Haures asked me how far I was willing to go for Sammael, I thought getting the ashbalm flower was some kind of weird test.

But if it only blooms for those in need... well, that

explains why it smelled like Mom's chocolate chip cookies. The ashbalm flower really was meant for me, but what about our mate bond? And what do they mean, 'interfere'?

"Exactly," agrees the duke. "And the only one that can use its magic is a bondmaster. Someone who can sense bonds—and someone who can *break* them."

Sammael's forehead furrows, the ridges on his brow standing out. "There hasn't been a bondmaster in Sombra in millennia. Definitely not during my existence."

"And that just goes to show that the professors don't teach their pupils everything in the School of Mages, do they? Because of course there's been a single bondmaster all along. How else would a demon like me take over the capital?" He grins, showing off his sharp tusk-like fangs. "There are worse fates than being banished to the shadows. Sometimes, just knowing such a fate is possible is enough to keep an entire realm in line."

Oh my... oh my *God*. Unless I'm wrong, the demon duke is basically admitting that one of the ways he tortures demons who rise up against him is by threatening to take their bonded mates from them.

Sammael's deep red skin pales, more of a dark pink than anything else. Yeah... I'm not wrong, am I?

He swallows roughly. "I... I did not know."

"You wouldn't, would you? Because, until now, you never had your mate, Sammael."

"Duke Haures—"

Acting as though my mate's voice hadn't turned pleading, the duke tilts the flower in my direction again.

His attention solely on me, Sammael's mouth clicks shut as everyone gathered waits on bated breath to see what Duke Haures will say next.

And, whoa, is it a doozy.

"With this ashbalm flower, I can break the bond between the two of you."

What?

Duke Haures pauses a moment for it to sink in.

Sammael's big body jerks, the chains rustling with the motion. The guard at his back digs his claws deeper into his skin, controlling him, while I'm a few seconds behind my mate.

And then I understand: the duke is threatening *our* bond now—and he's using the flower I risked myself to pick to do so.

My mouth falls open as my stomach twists. Did I really give the ruler of Sombra the one ingredient he needed to sever this new tie between me and my demon mate?

Yes. Yes I did.

Duke Haures makes a big display of sniffing the

ashbalm flower. I can only imagine what it smells like to him.

"It would be easy to do," he says. "Sammael would return to the dungeons and, in time, I might trust him again to serve as my mage. The mortal female would have to forget him and Sombra, of course, and I'd have another mage who knows the spell to perform it since Sammael clearly refused to." Another pause. A *calculated* one. "Or..."—or... or is good—"I could use the flower for something else."

It's obvious that he's talking to me now. I finally find my voice again to reply to him. "Like what?"

"It depends on your answer. Is Sammael your mate? Or is he my prisoner?"

I don't even hesitate. If I wanted to pretend like I'm not meant to be Sammael's mate—if I wanted it so that I *wasn't*—I could have stayed back in Westfield after the two demons took him away from me.

But I didn't. I went to Jericho, then I went to Sombra. I visited Nuit, Mavro, and the freaking shadows—and I did it all for Sammael.

I don't just want to rescue him from Duke Haures's clutches. I want to bring him home with me and continue what we started the night I taught him what a kiss... and *more...* could actually be like.

I want the forever he promised me.

I want—

HOPE

"I want him," I tell the duke firmly. "I... I *claim* him. If I'm his, then he's mine. Your gods said so, and you might be some bondmaster or whatever. I don't think you're a god."

Did I go too far? Possibly. But I'm right, and it's about time someone told the duke that.

After giving me an appraising look—and, in my mind, I'm already imagining myself being tossed back inside of the shadows with no escape this time—Duke Haures cocks his head, then looks at Sammael. "And what do you say to that?"

His purple eyes gleam more brightly than I've ever seen as he peers across the throne room at me.

Looking back at him, I don't see his fangs, his rust-colored skin, the ridges that stand out along his brow... I'm only vaguely aware that he's a foot and a half taller than me, that he could swoop me up in his embrace and make me vanish completely from either world.

At that moment, as I see all the love and affection written in every bit of his awed expression, I kinda feel like we have.

Sammael rumbles deep in his chest before he says out loud, "That I pity those who don't have Hope for their mate. There is none better, but they will never know because, now that she's claimed me, I will never stand for any to separate us again."

"Even I, my mage? Is that what you're saying?"

Duke Haures asks his question so conversationally, I almost forget that he has the authority to keep Sammael in those chains. If he decides on a whim to put him back in his dungeons, there is nothing we can do to stop him except see if he'd let me go with Sammael; at least that would be better than the shadows.

Because my big monster mate did get one thing right. They took him from me once, but I faced my fears and not only drove across state lines to find him —I went to a demon realm! I willingly walked into a wall of black shadows with glowing white eyes looking at me like I was lunch!

A stint in the dungeons with Sammael as my cell-mate? That spell I read—no matter why I did it—

promised me my true love. So what if my true love turned out to be a seven-foot-tall demon who shows his affection by bringing me acorns and watching over me while I sleep?

I meant what I said. He's mine, and I'm not going to leave his side. The only reason why he was sentenced to the dungeons in the first place is because he wanted his mate and was desperate enough to steal that old spell book, then spend four months haunting me.

He loves me. From the moment he found me in my dreams, holding out his hands while saying 'please', I think I already felt a pull toward him. It's only grown stronger since, and now that I know that when a Sombra demon says forever, he means *forever*... that the bond between a demon and their mate is so absolute that I'll never have to worry about human concerns like divorce or growing apart or any kind of cheating if Duke Haures doesn't use the ashbalm flower against our bond... I'm ready to open my heart up to Sammael the way I've already let him have my body.

Well, except for during the gold moon. I haven't changed my mind about being childfree and, luckily for me, everything I can sense about Sammael makes me realize that he feels the same. He just wants his mate, to honor her and to spoil her, to pleasure her and to keep her safe and protected—and, no matter what happens next, he has her.

Like I told the duke, if I belong to Sammael, he belongs to me.

Sammael shakes off the guard's hold. Surprisingly, Glaine lets him, staying motionless as my mate marches over to me.

Despite the chains keeping his hands bound together, he reaches out, swallowing up my fingers in his much larger, warmer ones. Without letting go, he glances over his shoulder, finding Duke Haures's vaguely amused expression.

"Yes," Sammael says simply. "The chains bind my magic. They keep me from turning to shadow. They take my strength, but when I hold Hope's hand in mine, I need none of that to know that I will sacrifice everything for my mate. Including my loyalty to you, my lord. I'm sorry, but from the moment I found Hope, she's earned it all. My essence was just the last part of me I gave her until I became hers and hers alone."

"Forget the bond for now. What if I banish you to the shadows instead of my dungeons? The first law isn't my only, as you know all too well. You stole from Sombra, Sammael. You stole from me. You risked your mate, and the other females. You risked *mine*. I've sent better males to the shadows for less."

Sammael gulps visibly before shaking his head royally, his long black hair settling over his shoulders. "Then I'll end this existence with her name on my chest and on my lips so long as you spare her."

Wait— *what*?

"Sammael." *End this existence…* like, *die*? He's supposed to be immortal—but does that mean he can't be killed? All those skulls… is that what's going on right now? Is Duke Haures threatening to execute him? Panicking, I squeeze his fingers, clutching them tightly. "No!"

It comes out more shrill than I intended, but what else could I do? I only just found him. The idea that I could love him and never worry about being betrayed, never *lose* him… and now this?

Sammael's head snaps back so that I have all of his attention. "Hope—"

It's in the way he says my name. It's in the way I'm tapped into him, even with the magic of the charmed chains working to close off part of our bond even without the ashbalm interfering with it. I already have his soul… his essence… whatever he wants to call it. His heart, too.

But he'll also sacrifice his life for me if he must, and he'll go to his end simply grateful that he had those few 'cycles' with me.

Good for him. Me? I had barely two days with him outside of my dreams and, sorry if I'm greedy as fuck, but I want *more*.

"You're my forever mate. My true love! That's how this is supposed to work, right? That's what Shannon said… and you, Sammael. You said, if I bond myself to you, you'll never leave me. You already did once. Don't do it again!"

"I do not want to, my mate—"

"So *don't*." He's being stubborn, the big idiot. I know what he's doing. Just like when he let Loki put him in chains, he thinks he's being all noble and protecting me.

Screw that.

Letting go of Sammael, ignoring the way I get a pang of both pain and remorse as though he thinks I've changed my mind and I'm rejecting him now, I turn to the duke.

Before I can say anything, though, Duke Haures lifts his hand. "Be at ease, female. I just had to make sure that, if I was losing my best mage, it was because he wanted to go and not because fate said he must. That is all. Forgive me, if you would."

I'm not the only one who is filled with confusion at the duke's comment—and sudden change of heart. I mean, I'm glad he's trying to calm me down—and he should, since he's the one who got me all wound up in the first place—but what is he saying now?

Sammael doesn't seem to know, either.

Chains clinking as he moves so that he's standing in front of me, forever protecting me, he says softly, "Your grace?"

"I've lived a long time," Duke Haures begins. "Longer than nearly every other demon on this plane. I know what it's like to be lonely, and to feel the relief when my one true mate is within my claws. But there are those who want what they believe is owed to them so desperately that they forget to see what's right in front of them."

His glowing blue gaze slides to the side. Standing next to the red-eyed shadow monster who seems to be *her* shadow is the same pretty brunette human woman who burst into the throne room earlier.

I finally know who she must be.

Su... she has to be Susanna Benoit, the first name scrawled in cursive on the inside of the *Grimoire du Sombra*.

Duke Haures's mate who went and retrieved an ashbalm flower of her own—but she's still here. Obviously. She found the flower and, whatever happened after that, chose to keep her bond instead of letting the magic in the ashbalm sever it.

Well, I can do the same thing, can't I?

Duke Haures's monstrous features soften as he looks at his mate, and I get the vibe that the story of their mating is probably even more complicated than mine and Sammael's. Even so, she's still here.

With all of us watching, she blows him a kiss. Around his fangs, the duke smiles.

He actually *smiles*.

It's gone by the time he turns back to face the rest of us. I know what I saw, though, and I'm feeling a million times better than I did a few seconds before as he clears his throat before shifting on his throne so that he can address my mate.

"You would never let go of your bond, Sammael," Duke Haures announces, surprising absolutely no one with his statement. "Your mate has proven that she has no intentions to, either. The gods have chosen well for the both of you. Who am I to stand in the way of such a pairing? The ruler of Sombra, yes, but you... you won't be returning to Sombra for quite some time, will you?"

I suck in a breath. If Sammael says that he wants to stay... I don't know what I'll do. After meeting Kennedy in Nuit—and Susanna in Mavro—I know there are at least two human women who live in Sombra among the demons and demonesses. They seem happy enough, but I... I can't do that.

I love my job. The idea of never seeing Johanna or her kids again? They'd never forgive me if I just up and disappeared, and it's not like I can explain where I'd be.

Kyle and Courtney are seven. They still believe in things like magic, but that doesn't mean they want Auntie Hope vanishing into another realm. I can't even fathom the idea of missing out on watching them grow up. I tease Jo about her driving all of the time and ask her what it will be like when the twins are old enough to get their licenses. I want to see that. I want to see all of it.

But I want Sammael, too.

Call me selfish, but Shannon made me think that I could have both…

Sammael locks on me, easing my nerves with barely a glance—and what he says next. "No, your grace. I will not… so long as you allow it."

"Me?" Duke Haures shakes his head. "You should be asking your mate if she'll allow you to return with her to her realm, not me, Sammael."

My mate still hasn't looked away from me. With that same expression he wore when he pushed his way inside of me that first time—a mixture of wonder, worry, and a desperate need to do this right—he murmurs my name.

That's enough for me.

"Yes. Of course you can!"

I finally give in to the urge to throw myself at him. I nearly trip over the chains in front of him, closing the small gap between us. Luckily, there's enough length between the cuffs on his wrists that he can open his arms wide enough to accept my trembling body within their grasp.

The chains jangle as he lifts his hand, running his claws through my hair. "I will be the best male for you, my mate," he murmurs. "I vow it."

I believe him.

"Let's go home," I whisper back, speaking against

his chest. Before the duke changes his mind... "I wanna go home."

Damn demon senses. I whispered, but Duke Haures still heard me, didn't he?

He clears his throat. The sounds reminds me of the old garbage disposal from my childhood home. "Sammael. Approach the throne."

I squeeze whatever part of him I can reach, not wanting to let go, but knowing I have no choice. Swallowing the sudden lump in my throat, I start to pull away from him.

His hand presses to the small of my back, keeping us connected. Then, guiding me to walk with him, he brings me toward the duke's throne so that I'm not standing by myself again.

Duke Haures doesn't say anything about that. Instead, he nods over our heads at Loki. "The chains. You may remove them."

Loki had stayed where he was even after the portal he created winked out and I stepped away from him. I had expected him to return to Nuit so that he could be reunited with Kennedy, though it makes sense when I remember that Loki's the one who put the chains on Sammael. With Duke Haures's permission, he joins us by the throne and waves both of his hands over Sammael's chains.

Each cuff unlocks at the same time. The metal of

the cuffs and the chain links connected to it *clink* as they hit the floor before vanishing entirely.

Duke Haures nods again. "That will be all."

Loki doesn't hesitate. Just like I thought, he immediately summons another portal. A moment later, he's gone.

So is that guard that had stood silently at Sammael's back.

I don't know when or where or how he disappeared, but he's gone.

Good riddance.

Susanna, however, has edged closer to her mate's dais, her shadow hovering even closer in case I decide to, like, bum rush her or something. I guess that, because she's the duke's mate, she gets her own bodyguard. I get that, but I'm not paying her any attention. Not really.

Oh, no. The only thing I'm focusing on right now is the way the ashbalm flower in Duke Haure's hold has suddenly gone up in flames.

I gasp. I can't help it. I worked so hard to bring that back here before I knew *why*, and I'm not sure how he did it—especially since he explained he's not a mage like Sammael and Loki, but a *bondmaster*—but the duke just freaking *incinerated* the flower. Hopefully that's a good thing, but excuse me if I'm just a bit bitter that all my hard work went up in flames like that.

The fire doesn't seem to bother him. In fact, the

source of it is definitely the duke because I can see the flames covering his palm, even licking down past his thick wrist as the flower burns.

Then, almost as quickly as the fire began, Duke Haures shakes his hand. The fire dies—and so does the ashbalm flower. No longer looking like a faded black carnation, it's nothing but a pile of actual greyish ash cupped in the duke's palm.

"Come here, Sammael."

He doesn't let go of me. Though the duke called my mate only, he brings me the rest of the way toward the throne.

This close, I can see the seven silver characters carved into Duke Haures's shockingly white chest; just like Loki and Malphas, he bears the name of his mate: SUSANNA.

Once we're within his reach, Duke Haures stands up from his throne. I have to swallow the 'holy shit' that nearly bursts free from me. He's even huger than the throne made him seem, and I feel so incredibly insignificant standing in front of him.

But then Sammael loops his arm around my waist, tucking me into his side, and that feeling fades as I turn into my mate, holding him close.

Duke Haures turns his cupped palm over Sammael's head, letting the ashbalm flower's remains rain down on him.

As it settles over him, the weirdest fucking thing

happens to the silver glyphs carved into his solid, red-skinned chest. It said 'SPES' before, I'd put money down on it, but the moment Duke Haures sprinkled the ashbalm flower's *ash* over Sammael, it's like the letters danced over his skin, reforming into 'HOPE'.

Now, just like the others, he wears *my* name.

I saw it. His gaze still geared upward, watching his ruler warily, Sammael didn't.

"The ashbalm flower failed, your grace. Our bond seems stronger than before if anything."

"Of course. Did you think I would go back on my word and remove it after your mate claimed you so boldly?"

Through the bond that's definitely still between us, I get the idea that Sammael had expected it when the duke called him forward. He went anyway because he didn't want to risk me being thrown in the dungeon—or the shadows—with him if that was to be his fate, but he brought me with him because the thought of letting go of my hand... he couldn't do it.

And now he'll never have to...

Duke Haures sits down again, leaning back on his throne, a self-satisfied grin curving around his tusks. "You love your female. I see that. I *sense* that, Sammael. But the spell that summoned you to her left you splintered, your bond weaker than it should be... there would always have been a part of you that doubted you were worthy of the same. You gave her your essence, but there were a few drops that lingered in the shadows. Now, it belongs completely to her." He gestures at Sammael's chest with his claw. "Your mate bond is unbreakable now. Not even I could sever it. See?"

Sammael glances down at himself. And, his fangs overhanging his lush bottom lip, he grins when he notices the change in his chest.

To see him smile like that while wearing my name proudly on his skin?

It might have been a major pain in the ass to get that ashbalm flower, and I had to bite my lip not to curse out Duke Haures when he offered to use it to break our bond or freak the fuck out when he set it on fire... but I don't regret my trip into the shadows now that it has solidified the bond between Sammael and me.

I don't regret it, not one bit.

EPILOGUE

HOPE

I know that this is just the beginning for Sammael and me, but as he waves his big hand, creating another one of those shadow portals like Shannon's mate and then Loki did, I get the feeling that this... this is also the happy ending I never thought I'd ever have.

I mean, there's so much we need to discuss. I want to ask him about my name on his chest and why it changed the way it did. Duke Haures mentioned that our bond is solid now—unbreakable—and I want to know why it wasn't before.

When it comes to forever with Sammael, what does *that* mean?

I still have the download of who he is in my brain. I

pushed it aside before because it wasn't so easy to tap into, but now that the ashbalm flower basically bolstered our bond, the answers are coming a lot easier.

Either that, or this is just me accepting for once and for all that I have claimed him as mine...

It doesn't matter. Through our bond, I know that, when he thinks of forever, he sees my face. That's all he wants. He wants an eternity with Hope as his immortal mate, and with Duke Haures's blessing to head back to Westfield, it looks like that's what he's going to get.

But even though I can pick answers out of the essence of who my demon mate is, that doesn't mean that I have *all* the answers. Right now, I have a million questions—but even they can wait since the one thing I want to do is ride Sammael like he's a freaking stallion.

We have forever, right? The rest can wait.

Just before he leads me through his portal, my mate's nostrils flare. Gazing down at me, his breath shudders out, and I remember the way he told me how delicious I smelled. He hadn't been talking about my body splash or my deodorant, either, and when he starts to rumble deep in his chest as he inhales again, I know he's not now.

His hand is a heated brand at the small of my back.

"Come, my mate," he says, the promise of all the pleasure that was cut short when the demon soldier interrupted us evident in his throaty voice. "Let us return to your home."

I circle his palm with my thumb, grinning cheekily up at him. "You mean *our* home, don't you?"

His body tightens. He's still in his solid form with the shadow-looking leathers covering his bottom half, but I'm sure if I slip my hand out of his and lay mine on his crotch, I'd find one hell of an impressive cock pushing against his shadowy clothes.

All the more reason to yank on his hand and drag him through the portal... which is exactly what I do.

I know I can only pull the seven-foot-tall demon behind me because Sammael allowed me to. I don't care. With his love and lust and desire for me rushing through our bond, with mine for him crashing into his, I can't wait to return home with my new mate.

I'm not sure exactly where I expected Sammael's portal to take us, but I'm glad when my ash-covered shoe steps down on a familiar carpet. He brought us right back to my living room, and I'm so glad to see my house that I don't notice the state it's in for a few seconds.

It's the door that catches my attention first. It's open. Not all the way, but there's a crack that let in the brisk autumn breeze.

Compared to Sombra, my house feels like an icebox. And though the wind had obviously seeped indoors, unless this was another Superstorm Sandy, there's no reason my house should look as ransacked as it does.

Drawers are pulled out, doors to a few of my cabinets visibly open. One of my dining room chairs is on its side. A couple of sheets of papers are scattered all over the floor. The horseshoe I kept posted over my front door is gone. So is the umbrella I keep hooked on the rack next to my keys.

And that's all I notice at first glance.

Sammael follows through the portal, landing right behind me. He hesitates for a moment, then asks softly, "Oh, my mate... what happened?"

I know the answer to that. "My house was hit. While we were in Sombra, I guess I was just another one who got broken into."

Sammael wraps his arms around my shoulders, spinning me around before tugging me close. His chin is nestled on the top of my hair. I probably smell like a mix of sulfur and dirt and who knows what else, but he doesn't say anything except, "I am so sorry."

I brace my hands on his sides. "Don't be, Sam."

I... I don't know why I called him that. It just slipped out, but the moment it does? It feels... it feels *right*. Like I thought of him as 'Sammael' when he was the demon I summoned straight out of my dreams. Now that he's real... now that I get to keep *him*... he's my 'Sam'.

Maybe he didn't notice. He's pretty distracted so

maybe he missed my slip—and then I hear him rumbling deep in his chest again.

He rubs my back in circles, obviously content. "You called me 'Sam'."

Yup. He noticed.

"You said I could," I remind him. "Remember?"

"I do. But you chose not to when we were mating even though... you see, Malphas's mate gave him a name of her own. 'Mal'. I thought that, perhaps, you could do the same. Thank you, my mate. It pleases me to be your 'Sam'."

He means it, too. Such a little thing to make him happy that, despite how frustrated I am that my house ended up being a target for the Westfield robber after all, I promise myself that he'll be 'Sam' from now on.

I can sense his emotions through our growing bond. So, it seems, can he when it comes to mine.

Pulling back so that he can look down at me, he says, "You are upset that someone entered our quarters while we were in Sombra. They took something that was yours."

His face screws up, concentrating. Releasing one hand from around me, he shows off a curved piece of metal. It looks like real silver, not iron, and it's more of a 'C' shape than a 'U', but it's undoubtedly a facsimile of a horseshoe.

"For you," Sam says, holding it out to me.

Oh, yeah. It's much heavier than the cheap knock-off I bought with Johanna at some tourist thing we went to a couple of summers ago with the twins.

My mate made it for me. I already love it.

Only—

"How did you do that?" I marvel.

"Simple. Thanks to our bond, I could sense what you had lost. I had no use of my magic while I was a phantom, but the ashbalm flower did more than strengthen our bond. I feel... I feel *whole* again, Hope. I'm myself again, and I owe it all to you, my wondrous mate."

Because I went into the shadows and gathered the ashbalm flower to repair our bond instead of break it...

It was one thing for him to tell me that he's a mage. Duke Haures made it clear that Sammael was a magic user like Loki was, but I guess I just thought of it as him being able to create portals, not conjure steel almost-horseshoes from thin air.

"That... that's amazing, Sam. What else can you do?"

"I can attempt to make my mate smile."

And then, before I can ask how he plans on doing that with my mess of a house surrounding us, Sam does exactly that when he uses my essence to pluck out the melody of my favorite song. In his alluring tone, he begins to hum Whiskey Rose's hit, "Heart Barely Used".

It's a break-up song, but I don't tell Sam that. The

fact that he's humming it for me means it's the most beautiful love song that's ever existed, no matter the lyrics.

He starts to dance, swaying with me. As we move, he switches from his solid form to his inky black shadowy shape. My fingers reach about an inch past the surface, tingling as I find the solid outline hidden amongst his shadows.

It feels *amazing*.

Sam lowers his mouth to my ear. Pausing in his humming, he murmurs, "And I can do this."

It's like the earth shifts beneath my feet. A gentle earthquake that makes me feel like I'm moving even if I don't actually *go* anywhere—and I think that I didn't until he puts a little space between our bodies and I notice that we're not on the first floor any longer.

Instead, my wily mate has moved us to my—*our*—bedroom.

One glance up at him and I don't need to be tapped into him to know what's on his mind. And as much as I agree, I remember what we left down there.

I scramble out of his reach before I let my hormones take over for my common sense. "Wait. The door. Downstairs... it was open."

It's a wonder the cops haven't been by yet. A door left open... did any of my neighbors notice? How long were we even gone? To me, it's still the same day I woke up with Sammael, then drove all the way to Jericho—

and, at some point, I'm going to have to figure out how to get my car back to Westfield—but how does time work across realms?

I don't know, but before I can ask him, Sam grins. He waves his hand, eyes becoming a darker shade of purple before he says, "It's shut. Locked, too. I've warded your entire house. Not even Duke Haures himself will be able to interrupt us now."

Well... in that case. I fall back into his arms.

He leads me to the bed. I'm more than willing to join him. I mean, I wouldn't say no to a shower right now—and I'm already thinking about how shower sex will blow my up-until-recently virgin mate's mind— but maybe a quickie to reinforce our bond is just what we need first.

However, right as I'm about to start slipping off my ash-coated jeans, my gaze happens to glance at my nightstand—and I immediately still.

Sam notices. "Hope? My mate?"

I point. "It's gone."

"Gone?" he echoes. "What's gone?"

"The book." It was on my nightstand. When I was getting ready to leave, grabbing everything I thought I might need, I plopped it down on my nightstand... then promptly left it behind. I remember that vividly— but it's not there now. "The grimoire. It's gone."

I'm crushed. Normally, I'd second-guess myself, thinking I misplaced it. But after the obvious proof that

I'd been burgled while I was in Sombra... it only makes sense that the same person who broke into my house stole the book.

I'm crushed—but my mate isn't.

"It was bound to happen," Sam says sagely.

"*What?*"

I could deal with the fake horseshoe tchotchke going missing, and for all I know, I left my umbrella at the library one rainy day and simply forgot about it. But the book... if it wasn't for that book, I never would have summoned Sam to me. Shannon seemed surprised that I'd left it back at my house instead of bringing it with me to Turn the Page. I hadn't meant to; I'd simply forgotten to grab it.

And now it's *gone.*

Sam plops down on the edge of my bed, pulling me onto his lap. I rest my head against his chest, looking at the **H** in my name as he trails his claws through my hair again.

"That's how the magic in the book works, my mate. No matter where it went or who took it, it will find its way to the next human destined for a Sombra demon."

"Like it did for us?"

He nods. "Yes."

I shift in his hold. I thought I felt something beneath me when he pulled me onto his lap. Moving just so, I'm sure of it—and, suddenly, I'm not thinking about that book any longer, am I?

And when I turn so that I'm straddling Sam, watching my name rise and fall as his breathing picks up while I shove him on the **O** and the **P**, pushing him so that he's on his back and I'm on *him*... I don't think he's worrying about the *Grimoire du Sombra* anymore, either.

---

*M*EANWHILE, SOMEWHERE IN *C*ENTRAL *N*EW *J*ERSEY...

He was almost done. The compulsion he'd been struggling to fight against for the past few weeks was beginning to ease up now that he had the old book in his hand, and once he sent it away, all of these midnight break-ins would finally end.

He found what he was looking for. The whisper inside of his head told him that he'd done well, and once he helped the charmed book toward its next destination, he would be rewarded.

Peace was all he was after.

He'd hoped the horseshoe would give him a little. Just like he pocketed other good luck trinkets during each of his searches, he'd removed the iron horseshoe from its post over the librarian's door before starting on the first floor.

Then again, maybe it *did* do something to help him achieve some peace. After all, it was the librarian's bedroom that held the book.

And now he had it—but he wouldn't for long.

The elderly woman standing behind the counter was smiling at him. Remembering himself, he forced his lips into something more like a grimace, but she didn't seem to mind.

"Got a package to send out?" she asked.

He nodded. Yes. And maybe once it was finally gone, he'd sleep without seeing those glowing green eyes glaring back at him.

Please, he thought. *Please let this be the one...*

The postal worker pointed toward the left. "Supplies are over there, dearie. Boxes. Tape. There'll be a bit of a charge, but we can get that book of yours where it needs to go."

He nodded absently, shuffling over to the counter that held everything she mentioned. After setting the book down, he reached for a box he thought would fit. With trembling fingers, he set it up, letting out a sigh of relief when the cursed book was nestled inside.

The tape was crooked by the time he was done, but it did the job. Grabbing a blank label, he slapped it on the front, then snagged one of the community pens.

He scrawled the old house in Madison as the return address; if anything, he'd know where to retrieve the book this time if it was lost.

He pulled out his phone. Blanching when he saw the deep, purple circles under his dark eyes reflecting back at him, he quickly entered the code on his phone.

His dark blond hair was standing in clumps from all the places he ran his fingers roughly through it. Scratchy stubble covered his chin, dotted with grey.

How long has it been now? Too long since he saw something he wasn't supposed to see. Would he ever *unsee*? He doubted that, but the only way he could make up for it was by doing exactly what he was told.

So he read the first spell on the page again like he'd been told to—only the second time he ever had—giving control to the magic that cost him *everything*.

A chance at reconnecting with his ex-wife. A chance to apologize to her for where he went wrong all those years ago.

A chance at ever seeing his daughter again—who wouldn't recognize him now even if he did.

And peace... all he wanted was *peace*.

His fingers were still shaking as he typed in his question—"Who is Whiskey Rose?"—in the search bar.

"Whiskey Rose is the stage name for Sierra Landry..."

Using the pen, he took his time to print the name on the label before returning to search another question so that he could complete it and, hopefully, finish with demons and magic and curses for once and for all.

"You can send fan mail for Whiskey Rose to the following address..."

I'm used to getting all sorts of fan mail — but a *spellbook*?

After an in incident on tour leaves me cooped up in my penthouse apartment, on vocal rest for the unforeseen future, with only my grumpy pet cat for company, I'm desperate for a distraction.

At my manager's suggestion, I do something I haven't done in ages: I go through my fan mail. There was enough of it to keep me occupied... but I only get through one bag before I find a package addressed to me.

To *me*. Not my stage name. Not the name I've gone by since I was sixteen, but my *real* name.

Color me intrigued

There's a book inside, an old leather-bound book that has me curious. Inside? There's something called a 'true love' spell that, in a whisper since I'm not supposed to be speaking, I read out loud.

Forget vocal rest. When a seven-foot-tall horned *creature* with glowing red eyes appears in my apartment, I scream so loudly that I think I scare *him* even more.

I get over it, though. After the life I've lived, I thought I've seen everything — but then I find out that Dagon is an immortal shadow demon, I'm supposedly his fated mate, and he thinks I should give up all the glitz and the glamour and the fame to live with him in his shadow world all because he's "claimed" me.

Well... I wanted a distraction, didn't I?

Claimed by the Creature is the fifth book in the **Sombra Demons** series. It tells the story of Sierra and Dagon, a bored starlet with an amusing outlook on life and the devoted demon who will do anything to make her smile...

!

I spent years trying to decipher the old spellbook I found... and I was drawn to the duke in seconds.

I found the book in a library when I was sixteen. For the next twelve years, I made it my purpose to figure out what it was about. I'd always been interested in languages, and it amazed me that this wasn't any one I could research about.

Until I figured out that it wasn't just one language. It had its roots in Latin, with at least five other languages thrown in the mix, and once I saw the pattern, it was easy to translate the rest.

I already knew it was a spellbook. The title—*Grimoire du Sombra*—gave it away. But what I didn't know? Was that, after reading the whole book, I'd find a true love spell... and that it would work.

I took all of the precautions. Probably more than I needed to, but it didn't matter. When the portal opened in my living room, showing me a realm that shouldn't exist, the most awe-inspiring creature I'd ever seen strode into my room.

Duke Haures, the ruler of Sombra—and, I discover, my fated mate.

Only... I'm human. His first law prevents humans from having any contact with demonkind in his realm. So what is he to do?

If your answer is to use magic to bring me back to Sombra with him, you're exactly right... and, before long, I'm more than happy to stay.

---

* *Drawn to the Demon Duke* is a prequel to the **Sombra Demons** series. It tells the story of Susanna, Amy's aunt, and how she became Duke Haures's best-kept secret.

Make sure to join my newsletter to learn more about this special prequel that will be serialized in weekly installments via my newsletter—for completely free!

KEEP IN TOUCH

Stay tuned for what's coming up next! Follow me at any of these places—or sign up for my newsletter—for news, promotions, upcoming releases, and more!

SarahSpadeBooks.com
Sarah's Newsletter
Sarah's Signed Book Store

facebook.com/sarahspadebooks
x.com/stressie
instagram.com/sarahspadebooks
amazon.com/author/sarahspade

ALSO BY SARAH SPADE

Holiday Hunk

Halloween Boo

This Christmas

Auld Lang Mine

I'm With Cupid

Getting Lucky

When Sparks Fly

Holiday Hunk: the Complete Series

Claws and Fangs

Leave Janelle

Never His Mate

Always Her Mate

Forever Mates

Hint of Her Blood

Taste of His Skin

Stay With Me

Never Say Never: Gem & Ryker

Bound by the Moon

Sombra Demons

Drawn to the Demon Duke*

Mated to the Monster

Stolen by the Shadows

Santa Claws

Bonded to the Beast

Fated to the Phantom

Claimed by the Creature

Grabbed by the Guard

Stolen Mates

The Alpha's Heart*

The Feral's Captive

Chase and the Chains

The Beta's Bride

Wolves of Winter Creek

Prey

Pack

Predator

Protector

Claws Clause

(written as Jessica Lynch)

Mates *free*

Hungry Like a Wolf

Of Mistletoe and Mating

No Way

Season of the Witch

Rogue

Sunglasses at Night

Ain't No Angel

True Angel

Ghost of Jealousy

Night Angel

Broken Wings

Of Santa and Slaying

Lost Angel

Born to Run

Uptown Girl

A Pack of Lies

Here Kitty, Kitty

Ordinance 7304: the Bond Laws (Claws Clause Collection #1)

Living on a Prayer (Claws Clause Collection #2)

Diamonds are a Witch's Best Friend (Claws Clause Collection #3)